UNTIL SHE GOES NO MORE AND OTHER STORIES

UNTIL SHE GOES NO MORE
AND OTHER STORIES

Beatriz García-Huidobro

Translated by Jacqueline Nanfito

WHITE PINE PRESS / BUFFALO, NEW YORK

White Pine Press
P.O. Box 236
Buffalo, NY 14201
www.whitepine.org

Acknowledgments:
This book was published in the original Spanish by LOM Editions, Santiago, 2013

Publication of this book was supported by a grant from the National Endowment for the Arts, which believes that a great nation deserves great art; by public funds from the New York State Council on the Arts, with the support of Governor Kathy Hocul and the New York State Legislature, a State Agency; with funds from the Amazon Literary Partnership; and with generous support from the College of Arts & Sciences and the Department of Modern Languages & Litertures at Case Western Reserve University.

The translator wishes to thank Diamela Elite for graciously offering to write the Inroduction, the contemporary Chilean artist Guillermo Lorca for granting permission to use an image from one of his paintings for the cover of this book, Dennis Maloney of White Pine Press for his dedication to publishing literature in translation, and to editor Elaine LaMattina for her meticulous attention to detail in the preparation of the manuscript for publication. And, as always, to the author, Beatriz García Huidobro, for the faith that she has placed in me as a translator, a constant inspiration in my work.

Printed and bound in the United States of America.

Cover painting: Detail from *Se llama* (*The Twins*)I, by Guillermo Lorca. Copyright 2003 by Guillermo Lorca. Used by permission of the artist.

Book design: Elaine LaMattina

ISBN 978-1-945680-56-4

Library of Congress Control Number: 2022930220

Contents

Preface

Diamela Eltit

The work of Beatriz García-Huidobro is part of the outstanding literature produced in post-dictatorship Chile. Her narratives, centered around women, memory, and identity, unfold in shifts between past and present. Her characters traverse a precarious, often oppressive, landscape, merely existing in an opaque, limited reality. These women and their harsh daily dilemmas take center stage as the protagonists of Beatriz's narratives. In spite of a perceptible fragility, these female characters resist, and sometimes thrive, despite the hardships and obstacles placed in their paths, obtaining a semblance of normalcy in their lives.

The author's poetic voice infuses and illuminates her stories. Her words glide effortlessly and seamlessly as she creates both the exterior and interior lives of her characters, revealing a plurality of meanings that underscore and amplify her texts.

Translator Jacqueline C. Nanfito has translated four of García-Huidobro's stories, *Hasta ya no ir*, *Marea*, *Fatiga de material* and *Jardín japonés*, for this volume. Her translations will not only introduce the narrative art of Beatriz García-Huidobro to English-speaking readers but will also contribute to a greater esthetic and cultural understanding of Latin American literature.

I take great pleasure in acknowledging this extraordinary translation by Professor Nanfito as a laudable and necessary contribution to the effort to illuminate and give voice to Latin American women writers, who have for far too long occupied a marginal position in Latin American literature.

A Brief Historical Note on the Stories

Elaine LaMattina

These stories take place in Chile during the 1970s. Chile had long been a stable democracy, although ruled by aristocrats who, along with several large U.S. companies, monopolized the lucrative copper mines; owned large plots of land; and permeated every social, economic, and political sector of Chilean life. In 1970, Salvador Allende, the candidate of the Marxist coalition Unidad Popular (UP) was elected president.

Allende enjoyed a triumphant first year, followed by two disastrous final years. The UP coalition believed Chile was being exploited by foreign and domestic capitalists, and the government began to socialize the economy, taking over foreign firms, oligopolistic industries, banks, and large estates. In 1971, by a unanimous vote of Congress, the government nationalized the foreign copper firms, which were mainly owned by U.S. companies Kennecott and Anaconda. Socialization of the means of production spread rapidly and widely. The government took over virtually all the great estates and turned the land over to the resident workers. By 1972 food production had fallen and food imports had risen, so the government used emergency legislation to allow it to expropriate industries without congressional approval. It turned many factories, some owned by U.S. companies, over to management by the workers and the state.

After the nationalization of the copper mines, the U.S. government of President Richard M. Nixon launched an economic blockade in conjunction with U.S. multinationals (ITT, Kennecott, Anaconda) and banks (Inter-American Development Bank, World Bank). The U.S. further squeezed the Chilean economy by terminating financial assistance and blocking loans from multilateral organizations. It is notable, however, that during 1972 and 1973 the U.S. increased aid to the Chilean military, which was unenthusiastic toward the Allende government.

Soon demand outstripped supply, the economy shrank, deficit spending snowballed, new investments and foreign exchange became scarce, the value of copper dropped, shortages appeared, and inflation skyrocketed, eroding previous gains made by the working class. A thriving black market sprang up. The government couldn't impose austerity measures on its supporters in the working class. Nor could it get new taxes approved by Congress or borrow enough money abroad to cover the deficit. The economy went into free fall.

The Right, on the defensive in Allende's first year, took full advantage of the situation, forging a Center-Right congressional alliance. This coalition blocked all UP initiatives, harassed UP cabinet ministers, and denounced the administration as illegitimate and unconstitutional, thus setting the stage for a military takeover. The Supreme Court and the comptroller general of the republic joined Congress in criticizing the executive branch for overstepping its constitutional bounds, while Allende's supporters continued direct takeovers of land and businesses, further disrupting the economy and frightening the propertied class.

A showdown took place in the March 1973 congressional elections. The opposition expected the Allende coalition to suffer losses, especially with the economy in a tailspin. They hoped to win two-thirds of the seats, enough to impeach Allende, but the fifty-five percent of the votes they received was not enough of a majority to end the stalemate.

In the aftermath of the elections, both sides escalated the confrontation and hurled threats of insurgency. Street demonstrations became almost daily events and increasingly violent. Right-wing groups called for a cataclysmic solution. The most militant workers formed committees in their neighborhoods and workplaces to press for accelerated social change and to defend their gains.

Conditions worsened in June, July, and August, as middle- and upper-class business proprietors and professionals called for Allende's resignation or military intervention. By mid-1973 the economy and the government were paralyzed. In August, the rightist and centrists undermined Allende's legitimacy by accusing him of systematically violating the constitution and by urging the armed forces to intervene.

On September 11, the military, lead by General Augusto Pinochet Ugarte, launched its attack on civilian authority. Allende died during an assault on the presidential palace, and a junta took over the nation. General Augusto Pinochet was installed as president. He dissolved parliament, banned trade unions, censored the media and unleashed a wave of brutal authoritarianism. Pinochet's government committed numerous crimes against humanity and instituted a reign of terror to purge Chile of leftists. According to Thor Halvorssen, president of the Human Rights Foundation, Pinochet's government disappeared 3,000 opponents, arrested 30,000 (torturing thousands of them) and forced 200,000 people into exile. Pinochet ruled as dictator until 1990, when democratically-elected Patricio Aylwin was sworn in as president.

See them again side by side. Not quite touching. Lit aslant by the latest last rays they cast to the east-northeast their long parallel shadows. Evening therefore. Winter evening. It will always be evening. Always winter. When not night. Winter night. No more lambs. No more flowers. Empty-handed she shall go to the tomb. Until she goes no more. Or no more return. So much for that. Undistinguishable the twin shadows. Till one at length more dense as if of a body better opaque.

—Samuel Beckett
Ill Seen, Ill Said

Until She Goes No More

Among the hills of the slopes along the coastal plain are my father's lands. It's amusing to me that it's called that. I never saw the coast from there. My sister, Esther, is familiar with the ocean. She arrives with the news that even the earth smells different and that from a distance you can feel the sound of the waves. She gives each of us a shell and teaches us to listen to the sound of the sea. It's a broken, remote sound, so distant that at times it disappears. I run my tongue over the shell. It's salty and smells somewhat disgusting. But I like it and want to know the ocean.

Here the landscape is immense. The sky over the hills is like an avalanche of clouds in shades of grey that move with the wind. It envelops the curve of this land, which is hardly touched by green and always covered with a blanket of dark, dry, and dreary dust.

Inside my home, the air's still. Neutral tones on the walls, sepia in the faces of the inhabitants. Clothing and suits are somber in color. Or they darken. I'm wearing a dress that's totally white. At the end of the day, the color will be dampened and darkened by the dust suspended in the air. I'll wait for a sunny day then take my dress to the tidelands, scrub it against the rocks, then hang it from a branch. I'll stay there for hours waiting for it to dry in the wind, listening to the sound of the sea. Then I'll tuck the shell under my dress and walk back home defiantly, smiling at the relentless wind.

I keep storage containers under my bed. Inside one of them is that dress. Waiting, waiting.

There are no longer parties. Families live far from each other and the town is even farther away. Funerals are the most important event, with the exception of when the rains fall and all access is cut off. My mother always goes to bid farewell to those who've died. She removes her apron and covers her shoulders with a shawl and walks for hours along wearisome paths covered with dust. At times, they make me accompany her. Our march is silent. We always carry something in our baskets. She doesn't know how to extend her hands if they're empty. I'm bored by wakes. There are never enough chairs and I always have to stand through the service. I hear the litany of words and prayers. I know them by heart, but I don't open my mouth.

I don't speak when my mother dies, either. My older sisters already have black clothing because they're older. They want me to wear a dress that was hers. I cry and scream. Amelia gives in and lends me her skirt and blouse and puts on that black dress I don't want to wear.

My face is puffy. I'm pallid. I know my face is whiter than ever. And if they were to see the skin of my body, they'd know my blood drags along inside me. It's difficult for me to walk behind the men who carry the coffin. Someone holds me up so I can continue. Some elderly women look at me and comment that it's a pity what I'm experiencing. They don't know that it isn't pain that has me beaten down. It's fear.

My mother has experienced stomach pain for days. She doesn't rest. The cramps come and go. Each time she's more hunched over as she works. I don't want to be alone with her. I never knew what to say to her and even less so now. But she's asked me to prepare the dough and I'll stay. She speaks without waiting for a response. She tells me how I should do things so I can later be a good wife. I don't respond. I don't dare tell her that I've decided not to be a wife. She's going to ask me what I'll do instead, and I won't have a ready answer. School drags along until sixth grade, and I'm not a good student.

I'm wrapping the dough when I feel the silent thud of her fall. She breaks into a profound and hoarse cry and remains on the bare floor. She's listless. I look at her. I know that I should do something. I try to lift her up but I can't. My brothers are in the fields sowing. My sisters have gone to take lunch to the men and won't return for at least an hour. Even that's very improbable. The two of them have boyfriends and they get sidetracked and have fun among the thickets. They took the horses in the morning. If I let Aunt Berta know, surely she'll begin to scream at me. And maybe she'll run around saying horrible things about me. They're going to blame me, and it's not my fault that she fell. It's almost time for me to go to school. I'm no longer thinking. Nobody's going to know I saw her collapse. The others will know better what to do. I grab my notebooks and run to the road. I know that I'm screaming, but there isn't anyone who can hear my wordless cry.

Amelia has enormous hands. She's slender and moves gracefully while she's helping with the tasks. But she has these immense hands, where veins surface in an aggressive manner and traverse winding paths.

At times she hums songs. I can't determine if they're from the same time period as those our mother knew. Her voice barely achieves the level of the voice of the wind. Fragile as it is, it possesses a range of innumerable tones that seem to stroke and caress the shoulder, skin, and hair. When Jose began to wrap himself around her, no longer did her voice interrupt. She must think a lot about him, because when she's alone, she blushes in the same way she does when they're together.

The wake commences before the sun has all but lost itself among the hills. The sky turns crimson and the horizon is magenta, like the extended wings of a bird. The coffin hasn't yet arrived, nor have my father or my older brothers. There's no one to greet those who are arriving. I watch them and allow them to enter. They question me, but I don't know anything. They sit down around the table. When all the chairs are occupied, they arrange the furniture to accommodate the others. The women bring food to share. The men remain standing next to the open door. My father and brothers arrive carrying my mother. It's a silent, solemn entrance, like that of a bride entering the church. Only in this case, no one's smiling.

My father instructs Amelia to attend to those present. He asks nothing of me. She obeys and an aunt helps. They carry in a large tray with drinks, passing, retrieving, washing and passing once again. It's a silent task. Esther also helps serve. She offers the tray and the women react with suspicion. They pause before taking what's offered to them. They divert their glances upon taking a glass and drinking avidly. They murmur something

17

among themselves. The murmur increases when Esther serves the men. They examine her from head to toe with lustful eyes, seeking an invitation with each movement.

Soon they forget that my mother's there in the center of the room, withering away among so many flowers.

There's a photo of my family on the wall. Except that I'm missing. I'll be born some six years later, after my brother, Jaime, dies and nobody cares anymore about photographs.

They seem so serious, as if intimidated by the camera. Except Esther. She's a young, beautiful girl who seems to be leaning on the edge of the photo, her arms crossed and her gaze fixed upon the lens that's focused upon her. Her hair is light in color and her mouth is wide. She stops running down the slopes of the pastures when she becomes a young lady and then is no longer a lady when she becomes a woman. That's what they tell me when she chases after the man who deceived her. I regret that she takes off and makes light of the matter. Only my father laughs with her.

Now she visits whenever she feels like it. She knows the city very well and even the capital. She's seen the sun set over the sea and how it appears on the other side of the mountain range. She's worked in houses with floors that glisten like crystal. She's combed the hair of women with soft, blond hair. She's slept between luxurious silk sheets. She's read the letter from the founder of Santiago that's carved into an enormous stone at the base of the hill. She's experienced tremors without fearing the walls will collapse. She's wandered down streets filled with pedestrians where no one knows her. She's met many men in the city. They've taught her the secret to not having children.

The women speak ill of her. When Esther isn't here, words hang suspended in the air. But when she arrives and walks among the fields defying the wind, and the trees bow to her presence, no one speaks of her.

Each day I have to cross the pasture to get home. I run the entire way. Once I imagined the devil was pursuing me and I couldn't shake that impression. As I run through the wind, it grasps me and envelops all of my body in a frightful way. As I approach the gate, I begin to slow my frenetic pace. He's always there. I know he'll never not appear. It would be futile to try to evade him. So I pass by his door, walking with an air of distraction. Don Victor smiles from the threshold. I feign surprise upon finding him in his habitual place. And I smile with an uncontrollable grin.

"Come," he tells me.

But he could remain silent and I'd follow him, regardless of the interior of that cold and colorless house. Before he'd ask me things while his hands explored my legs. Not anymore. As soon as I enter, he embraces me and his urgent hands advance along my body. The wind howls in the distance. The sun, upon setting, brings a dazzling new radiance that expires upon appearing. A dense, grey twilight enshrouds the closed windows. The dust has already lifted when I leave.

"Don't say anything to anyone," are his parting words.

I walk away with my notebooks in hand and no longer run. I'm counting the coins he's given me. I'll bury them later in the hiding place with the others.

It can't be all that long. So many temptations at this age. And I'm still not yet twelve years old.

I tell him that I'm going to grow up. He tells me that he hopes that isn't so. His desires are much stronger than the forces of nature because my body isn't changing.

The sundowns are sluggish. The sun slips wearily behind the hills. At its highest point, it begins to set. Amelia finishes her work and leaves with everything prepared for the arrival of the men. Sometimes she manages to meet up with Jose, running toward the thicket of hawthorns. And there are some days when my brothers and my father arrive before she has the opportunity to get away. Amelia tends to their needs in silence, while the density of the sunset blends with the heaviness of the evening.

I approach the hawthorns. Jose has his head lowered and at times looks up with an expectant gaze.

Winter is approaching. They're thinning the thickets and Jose no longer comes.

One morning I awake covered in blood. I squeeze my thighs, but I'm not able to contain the sticky substance emanating from my body. Amelia tells me that I'm now going to grow and that I'll have the body of woman. Her large hands wash me gently. Then she cuts some cloth and shows me how to hide my shame.

Before afternoon falls, I walk to his house. I haven't gone to school or run through the pastures. He's seated in front of his desk, books and numbered papers in impeccable order. He removes his eyeglasses and looks at me more with curiosity than with surprise.

I tell him that there's something that I shouldn't show him.

I raise my skirt while he removes the precautions taken by Amelia. He introduces his fingers and they become drenched in the sticky liquid. On my belly he draws red and serpentine roads. Then it's my hand that becomes lost in that humid and profound tunnel. But the traces of my fingers on his skin swiftly disappear.

The cemetery is a hollow in which stones and crosses become confused. The wind devours and deflects them. Above the hole in which we buried our mother, my brothers have carved a wooden headstone with the face of the Virgin. Around the burial niche, Amelia has made a pathway of flowers. They are so few and so withered that we placed white stones among them. My father carries a jug of water so we can keep them growing.

Each week we make the long, arduous journey carrying the water but the withered flowers end up dying. The stones lose their color and are thinned among the dry branches. The rain soon begins and we end up leaving.

The following spring, Amelia gathers an immense bundle of branches of myrrh. I don't want to go, but her subdued gaze from behind the tiny yellow flowers convinces me. Jose no longer visits. They say he's after one of the daughters of don Licho. His parcels of land are much larger than ours and his animals are so numerous that they bump into one another.

I lift the water vessel and we begin the march. There's still mud, compounded by the dry dust that complicates the air. We encounter other visitors. Amelia greets them briefly and amiably. I simply remain silent, tethered to her shadow.

The cemetery is a quagmire. There's no longer is a pathway of flowers and stones. Rain and the wind have aged the face of the Virgin.

Someone broke the earthenware jar. We try to put it back together, but it no longer holds water.

Amelia examines with desolation the branches of myrrh. No one brings flowers amymore. Nor does she have anyone to whom to offer them. Amelia confesses to our father her fears. She knows her hands are large enough to cradle children and that her voice would be melodious to the ears of a child soothed by a lullaby. She doesn't speak of the desires that torment her sleep.

"A woman is needed in the house," he responds.

They don't even look at me. My scrawny and silent silhouette is enough of an argument for uselessness.

Esther left after the funeral and it's pointless to try to bring her back. She comes and goes like the winter storms, but each arrival is anticipated and welcomed with the anxiousness of the first signs of life from the earth.

My father seeks to console Amelia, assuring her that once one of our brothers is married, she'll no longer have to bear the weight of so many obligations. She nods and lowers her gaze.

Spring gallops among the hills and when summer comes, Amelia will turn twenty-three. There is no longer hope, simply impatience.

My mother gave birth to four men. Today there are three brothers that help my father in the struggle against the drought that follows winter, the devastation of the rains, the animals' loss of weight, and the sadness the dust leaves on the tenuous steps of man upon the earth.

Esther tells my brothers that in the capital there are families that possess thousands of acres like ours. And they consider them useless. They abandon them for their animals to graze. Or they invest in them, planting pines that will bring wealth to their grandchildren. They possess them and don't even mention them. And my poor father expends his health on these squalid parcels of land without a horizon.

Esther's chatter is as easygoing as her laughter, but she sews in it the root of bitterness, that vine that winds itself down the skin of men and emits a venomous secretion, making them confuse the sweat of their labor with the hidden tears of humiliation.

I barely speak to my father. At the table, he hunches over to sip his soup. The thick skin of his fingers cuts through the bread he dunks in his tea. While he chews his food, the fissures in face become more profound and obscure.

When he rises to leave the table, he regains his posture with a sense of pride. A glance at the hills erases the furrows in his face. He summons his sons to return to work and they leave together.

Only I know that in his commanding voice there lies the certainty of a man transcended by the blood and sweat he leaves on the earth.

There are three classes in school. There's a director and a couple of younger female teachers. They group us according to age, strengths, and limitations. If a student advances beyond the scope of the village, the director speaks with her or his parents. She exhausts herself trying to convince them to send her or him to San Juan, the largest town in the valley where diverse hamlets like ours are created and nurtured.

The families listen respectfully to the director. Her extravagant words extoll the intellect of the youth, clarifing and convincing the parents that school has finally ended and they once again have two hands to help with the work.

Sundays we go to church. Families begin congregating along the long and dusty road. Sometimes groups of young men ride in a cart pulled by oxen. They invite the young, single women, who look at their mothers with pleading eyes hoping for their permission, to join them. Almost always they agree, but often a couple of older women also climb on board.

My father walks arm in arm with Amelia. The young men don't bother to call out to her. Nor does she attempt to free herself from her father's grasp.

They don't invite me. I walk slowly along the trodden, worn path. Every Sunday this spring I've worn my white dress. The fabric clings to my body and the petticoat rubs against my legs.

Father Benito opens a worn Bible. It takes him a while to find the page due to the uncontrollable trembling of his hands. He begins a reading and I escape to the door. I cross the plaza and I'm in don Victor's store. At that hour, no one stops by to purchase anything. I go behind a counter as high as my shoulders. He allows me to reach down into the barrels. My favorite is the one with toasted wheat. I've already lost my shoulders and face in the barrel, when I feel his body pressing mine against the studded wooden barrel. His breath and mine cause a frenzied flurry of flour.

I shake myself off before climbing the steps to the church. I sit in one of the pews in the back. Dampness slides down my legs and adheres to my white petticoat. While we're given the final blessing, I hold tight to my pockets, filled with sweets and coins.

Before summer begins to sunder springtime, and the children no longer go to school in order to help out in the fields, we're going to make our First Communion. I finally learned the obligatory parts of the catechism and will be part of this year's group.

The girls have to wear a white dress with a cerulean blue tie around the waist. We all wanted a white, transparent veil. Miss Eugenia hears our murmurs. She explains the Lord is flattered and touched by simplicity and is offended by any ostentation, that our pure souls, in prayer and contemplation, are all that he expects from those who receive his body for the first time.

From his shop, don Victor sends meters of white chiffon to San Juan. He delivers them solemnly and ceremoniously to the director, in homage of her labor of sacrifice and unselfishness. He expresses the hope that the young girls will be radiant in honoring their school and the church of our small but dignified Pedregal.

The mothers sew the girls' veils. We stay after class making floral crowns from a cold clay that we form carefully. At sunset, Amelia picks up and polishes my work until I have the most beautiful of the crowns.

The day before the ceremony, don Victor gives me a pair of white lace gloves. The other girls are envious even before we join the solemn procession. I don't allow any of them to touch the gloves.

"They belonged to my mother," I say.

En route to the altar, my head held high and the rosary clutched tightly between my hands in the lace gloves, I know they're seeing me as different from the others.

When Father Benito asks us to respond in unison to the prayers, I realize that I've forgotten the words of the catechism.

Aunt Berta is my father's sister. She doesn't own any land and her sons have left to become laborers, to fight for wealth in the soil of others. She divorced her husband, who didn't know how to provide for his family. For a while, she lived with us. I was barely walking and I already distinguished her strident voice over the sweet, soft words of my mother, the ruckus of my siblings, the wind beating against the boards of our house, the rain sliding among distant trees and over stones scratching out an existence in the soil. Up close, her voice was relentless. She pointed out the sins of others with the precision of a jackal attacking her prey. She scrutinized, dug, and sniffed out the situation. Then she tore it apart. She strolled with the shreds of her destruction, smiling and jubilant. And then the tone of her voice lowered. From the depths of her chest there emerged, in a hoarse vibration, the reason for the punishment, the reason for the wrath of God, the terrible offense. She didn't know any victims, only sinners atoning for their guilt.

She now lives with her married daughter, not far from us. It doesn't matter where she is. Her entanglement extends itself and engulfs everyone.

The blows that life has dealt her, however, are signs from God to strengthen and affirm her profound and unyielding faith.

I receive the gifts with my lace-gloved hands. I set them aside and extend my lace-covered hands. I offer my cheeks instead of bowing my head. The other girls' crowns have either fallen off or tilted to one side. Mine remains firmly attached and encircles my head like an aura, with the veil falling gracefully, impeccably.

Aunt Berta doesn't offer me a gift. She tells my father to stifle my excessive pride before it overflows and drags me along a muddy, murky road like the one Esther took, one that arrives at the very entrance to hell and eternal punishment. My father raises his tired eyes to look at me. My head is lowered and my shoulders are hunched forward upon my sunken chest.

"She's a child," he tells her. And he smiles at me with the clumsiness of one who attempts to pull weeds out of dry soil or meat from a starving animal, but he's incapable of extracting even a sign of emotion from his heart, so close yet so foreign.

I return the smile, my brows arched and my eyes fixed on the lace of my gloves, my hands resting on the whiteness of my skirt.

If I could fly like a bird, I'd head toward the west. I'd see the hills rising and descending with a blanket of aridness until, dizzy from the swaying, I'd finally alight on the salty shore of the ocean. When I finally tired of feeling the warm sand on my skin and my eyes grew weary from watching how the sea foam erased the damp traces of my steps, then, my body stiff and whitened by the salt, I'd resume the flight.

I'd ascend to the highest of heights as I passed over my town and the undulating tracts of land that some former government had sold to local landowners that, for generations, had defied its barrenness. Perched upon the clouds, I wouldn't see Sauzal or El Paso, with their earthy plazas, rickety roofs and the confused, weary walk of men and animals, no longer distinguishable.

I'd descend to the sound of the river that flows from the other mountain range to the sea, the river that deviates and narrows its flow and doesn't reach our hills. My feet would touch the soft, green stretch of the valley and my eyes wouldn't comprehend the extension of so much fertile land. It would be a long, but never tiring, journey along the plain. It would take me hours to arrive in San Juan. My dress would still be white, perfumed by the morning dew and the fresh breeze. In the large town, I'd lose myself among the streets, the throngs of people, and the open air markets. I'd never want to return.

One time, Esther brings a mirror. Among the barren walls there appears an opening of light. At first, Amelia smiles at it and approaches it silently to adjust her hair. Then she wavers at the reflection of her weary figure.

I stand in front of the mirror. They've placed it too high for me. I can only see myself down to my thighs. So I take a chair, and while standing on it, I'm able to see myself completely. My dress slides down and what is revealed are the chest and the hips of a young man. Nothing is insinuated or nascent in the skin that clings ever so tightly to the scant flesh that covers my bones. Undressed and with my hair pulled back, I look like any one of the many peasants that run after their sheep in the hills. But when I loosen my dark hair, which falls like a blanket of rain upon the whiteness of the delicate body trying to balance on the wicker chair, the mirror speaks to me of the seduction found in ambiguity.

The men speak of the valley and their gaze strays toward our forever curved horizons. Some young men defy their elders and take off to become day laborers. For others, there's no alternative but to leave the land toiled by their ancestors. They've inherited their pride, but not the lands.

They're different when they return. Everyone gathers around them to try to experience that life, open and emergent like that of a thistle. My father says this is temporary, that time will soon bend their backs and expend their efforts. Then they'll see the emptiness in their hands and in those of their children. Other families reaffirm what he has to say. The fire extinguishes slowly. Several sons surrender. The embers reflect their diminished silhouettes, their heads turned toward the east.

Sheared wool inundates the houses at the end of spring. Before the water becomes just a lone, wavering trickle seeping through a crevice, the women wash pile upon pile in enormous baskets. Then young girls weed through the dry and dusty mounds. They carry pieces of opaque, amorphous whiteness and with their expert fingers, they spin, twist, and wind it around their spindles. It's hot and dust hovers around their eyes and mouths. That's why the songs of women are so soft and guttural.

Aunt Berta's hands are swift as serpents among the rocks. Intent upon her chore, she never ceases to chatter. Among the groups of women, she occupies the most prominent place. Nothing evades her, nor is there any decision made without her intervention.

The afternoon is heavy. The air is sweltering. Her words slice through it.

Doña Herminia's daughter slips away and escapes to the hollows with my brother, Pedro. Nothing chaste nor honest can come of the furtive steps of two young people. It's her duty to warn Doña Herminia of the risks that come with unbridled instincts. The latter is blushing. She's seen Pedro grow up. She recalls her youth when she looks into the luminous eyes of her daughter.

She follows her one day. She sees them embrace with desperation. Her daughter is resting her head on his bare chest when Doña Herminia interrupts them. She screams at them and shoves her toward the miserable ranch. The sound of her strikes seems to reverberate like the shrill sound of a tuning fork. The young girl repents. And asks for forgiveness. Her words ring hollow in the ears of her mother, and her hands unleash rage upon the daughter, out of shame.

Pedro's not allowed near Rosita. She's laying there, recoiled on the well-trodden earth, emitting a hoarse lament. He enters the house, panting.

Amelia's mending clothes. I'm knitting. Every season of the year, I can be found with knitting needles and a skein of yarn hanging from my lap. It's the only domestic task I've learned. Pedro tells us what has happened. His eyes are glistening. His voice breaks. I think he's going to cry. I've never seen tears roll down a man's cheeks. He finishes his brief story amidst the rapid and harsh din of my knitting needles and the movements of Amelia preparing some scraps of cloth, a bottle of alcohol, and a clay crock.

We leave our brother halfway down the road. I want to stay behind with him. I have an uncontrollable desire to see him cry, to understand outright the difference between the suffering of women and men. Amelia insists she needs me. We stop for water, which I carry. The vessel becomes cool and I hold it tightly against my tummy. It's refreshing. And pleasant to the touch. With this sweet, satisfying sensation I enter the home Doña Herminia.

Rosita is sprawled upon something that resembles a filthy straw mattress. She's trying to reach something with her hand but she isn't able. Amelia helps her recline. She tells me to bring dirt in a washbasin. She dampens the cloth in alcohol and rubs her face. She then prepares a clay poultice and applies it over her body as she undresses her. She's a robust young woman, but upon removing her garments, the skin spills over in soft white mounds. She's bruised.

"So many," I murmur. One side of her face is swelling above her lips.

Amelia's hands are swift and precise. Rosita is now breathing easier, less agitated. Amelia tells her that the blood is washed away and the bruises will soon disappear. But the blow to her honor is singular. And fatal. Indelible.

Amelia's words sound like those of Aunt Berta. The tone is somewhat different, but tangential. Soon they'll sit down next to one another to toss around venomous words disguised as morality, to conceal and soften the harshest poisons. I ask her not to talk that way. She glances at me with her habitual tenderness.

"I don't understand you," she replies. I embrace her and I ask her, I beg her, to never be like Aunt Berta. Clearly she doesn't understand me. She thinks I'm overwhelmed by what happened to Rosa. While returning home she calms me with her soothing voice, transformed into the voice that belongs to another. With the voice of women who don't have a male's body to stretch out next to; after an exhausting day's work they don't have a chest upon which to rest their head and nap until relaxation reaches the climax of the senses. Women that fall into their worn, narrow beds totally spent, their arms outstretched and their nightgowns closing tight around their necks, stifling in their throats the silenced sighs that never were.

"Amelia," I tell her, you have to go. "Go on. You still have time," I insist.

There are three of us sisters. It's as though we were conceived in different seasons and born with the moon in different phases. Esther is like a joyous and mighty river that hums along a specific course. Or the verdant and incommensurably wide ocean, that from the heights of its descent, surely dismisses anything in its wake with a permanent smile and a gaze that never looks back.

Amelia is like the earth, clinging tightly to her ground. She wants to be sown, to blossom and then be cut and gathered beneath the shade of the same tree. And sought out by the same hands, bending under the weight of the same feet. To look at the sky from the lowest of depths and see in the rich gamut of grey subtle differences, without ever knowing that despite that contrast, they're similar: black and white before they fused into one.

I resemble the wind that slides silently but howls if it's detained or interrupted. The wind that never ceases in its relentless attempts to slip away, though it doesn't know where it's going.

In El Paso there's an annual fair. Six days of summer, six days of parties, six days of oblivion. The peasants take what they've managed to extract from their lands, their animals, and their hard-working hands. I take all that I've knitted in a year. Caps, vests, shawls in a coarse wool. Under the dusty sun, none are attractive to anyone whose reddened eyes glance down to see what I'm offering on a blanket spread on the ground.

The austerity of the women, their recollection of the cold and the wind, makes me finally let everything go for less. I give some of my earnings to my father. Some I use to purchase dyed wool with which I'll enhance the next knitted works. The rest of the money dances among my fingers, safely kept in the pockets of my white dress. There are lovely things, brought from San Juan: fabric, transparent glass objects, plates of many colors, sausages made from smoked ham, crystal wine carafes, herbs to cure the illnesses of the body and mind.

But the place where I inevitably end up is the stand of doña Esmeralda. I don't even know if that's her real name. She's a red-headed woman, with an attitude that's only attainable in the city after knowing its secrets. She's reclined on a carved wooden chair, sideways to her merchandise, indifferent to her customers. In her hands she cradles something that she raises to her eyes, moving almost imperceptibly. I approach her stand, keeping a prudent distance, as the brightness of the stones of her jewelry is overwhelming. The settings are stunningly artful and totally different one from the other. Even if I had a million coins and could choose any one of those jewels, I wouldn't be able to decide which one to select. I spend hours looking at what I cannot afford. At times, doña Esmeralda glances at me and smiles.

28

Among her front teeth she has gold-plated inserts that illuminate her mouth and make her smile radiant, and I no longer wait for another smile.

She tells me to approach. I'm wringing my hands behind my back. She doesn't leave her chair, but the expression in her eyes and the sweetness of her voice are more inviting than if she had taken me by the arm.

I allow myself to run my fingers along the cool metal. Something is set in motion and runs through my blood when I feel that foreign contact.

"Try them," she insists.

I remain immobile. I hear something escape from my mouth. Unintelligible words, excuses for not having the necessary money. She slides out of her chair and places a necklace around my neck. On my wrist she places a bracelet whose jingle is similar to that of a distant river. The earrings she places on my ear lobes begin to sway softly, rhythmically. Some of the rings seems to immobilize my hands. Doña Esmeralda places a mirror in front of me and I can't contain a sigh. I so profoundly regret the stark contrast between my listless body and that unattainable brilliance.

Amelia is next to the bags of ground corn. She prepares packages of dried corn flour. There are always fewer than anticipated. After setting aside that reserved for the family and for paying for the mill, there's barely anything left to sell. The aroma is the aura of my sister at the fair. I tell her I've come to invite her to see doña Esmeralda's jewels. She's not interested.

"Only men who are engaged to be married should get close to those jewels. A young single woman should wait until the man approved by her father can entice her with them. A decent young woman would never wear them. Besides, you shouldn't speak with that woman," she warns me.

I want to know why, but Amelia doesn't offer explanations. I suspect she doesn't even know the reason. But to approach doña Esmeralda is akin to committing an imprecise crime.

It's summer. Warm afternoons that barely begin. Everyone stretches out in the shade of the trees. A nap among the thickets. I head to the stream to cool off. I untie my hair to wash it in the stream.

Before I immerse my head, I see her. She's off in the distance. A man is accompanying her. They stare at me. I know she's speaking about me while he nods his head. I pretend not to have seen them and begin to scoop up water in my hands. I splash my skin indiscriminately but slowly. Each movement is for their benefit. It's my body that's spinning, set into motion, but its that distant stare which is provoking the movement.

Doña Esmeralda approaches. The gentleman turns around and takes off. I don't stop playing with the water until her voice reaches me. It's impossible to understand the words she sings into my ears. I straighten out my skirt and simply follow her.

The house is located on a dusty street. The façade is made of adobe. There are no windows, only a wooden door worn from woodworms. We enter. It's refreshing and dark. Doña Esmeralda ceases the encouragement she'd been giving me, changing the soft, sweet words to a glacial stare.

At the end of the room is a doorway from which a curtain hangs. The man appears there. He's shirtless. He smells of a dank, musty humidity. He tells me to enter the room, where there's a rickety bed. I sit there with my eyes fixed on an iron sink with a ceramic basin filled with water. They briefly murmur something between them. The man gives her something. I should know what it is, but I don't. If I no longer remain there, if I flee, I'll be running toward the immutable. In the immobility and the silence I find action and immediate change.

The man draws the curtain and approaches me. His waist is eye level. He unzips his pants and tells me that I am now going to know what a man is.

There are several men who want to be the first to introduce themselves into a young girl's body. Doña Esmeralda tells me it will always be the same. A motionless body, eyes wide in panic from feeling how this new path opens and eventually clears, contractions under the skin. Drown the cries of pain against his chest, but don't smother them so much that they become inaudible. Awkward hands. Everything distant.

In the shadows of the room, her smile no longer glistens. The gold has changed to copper. Well-worn bronze protecting the grotesquely painted lips.

I don't mind if they eliminate themselves inside of me. Nor that they exhale and whisper into my ears miserable words and sighs. Not the sweat of their anxious bodies nor the heavy weight of the satisfied.

It doesn't matter to me if their skin is tight and luminous or if it's been carved by time. Their facial features contract in the same way and their hands apply pressure exactly the same, with an identical rhythm of intensity, whether they've worked the land or licked and sealed documents.

I don't waste time determining if the words spoken are obscene, violent or tender. They all erupt from the interior to spill out over the very entrails that vomit them. The need for flesh created by flesh, returning to itself.

I wouldn't recognize the face of the gentleman into whose body I melted yesterday, what he confided in me, how many fears he allowed to escape, how much perversity he allowed to escape, how much pain he'd been hiding in his silence.

But the scent that encircles the neck of every man is always distinct and each one singularly repulsive.

Night is already closing the windows. I have to leave. Doña Esmeralda speaks to me, drawing aside the curtain. She tells me to wait a few minutes. She smiles: *This one is going to be sweet.* Behind her is a young man. He's just like my brothers, but he smiles with the abandon of one from the city, looking straight into my eyes, approaching in a way that makes the distance seem more pronounced.

He's thin. Solid. His muscles are long and flexible. His skin is soft, almost hairless. He's clean, almost smelling of some sweet fragrance. The timbre of his voice turns his words into silver, as if burnished by a silversmith. He talks a lot. He questions even more. About my age, why I'm here, about the future, about the parcels of land, about what moves my soul. He gives me advice in a tone that's low and cadenced, while his hand slides through my hair and then along my body. He has taken my hands in his and gently caresses my fingertips.

"Don't speak" he tells me.

Even though it's dark, I can see his gaze and he can see mine. I say nothing. His words have burst forth only after his urgency has been satiated.

In Pedregal every family prepares their own bread. The dough rests a few hours covered by a white cloth. Then it's placed into a clay oven, from which no odor escapes. Upon removing the steaming bread, the vapor mingles with the suspended dust and it's as if the air becomes baked. Immediately the women smother the scent by wrapping the men's nourishment in cloth. Tethered to the heavy satchel, the women leave their houses hurriedly to deposit the fruits of their labor upon the table outdoors.

31

The towns have their bakeries. From the threshold of the door a white flag hangs and sways rhythmically to the waves in the air emanating from the ovens. In the house next door to one in which doña Esmeralda has given me shelter, there are skilled bakers. The smell that for hours has been enclosed in the room blends with that the neighbors produce in their own ovens.

It awakens the mens' appetites.

I no longer eat bread.

In winter, the women's hands become reddened by chilblains. In the spring, their hands recuperate in form and color, becoming an almost rosy white. Caresses abound then. It's almost as though childbirth ends up happening in a season of rain.

With spring, women remove their shawls and their coarseness.

With summer, they're undressed. Flimsy fabrics cling to their figures. Disheveled tresses sway over their backs and shoulders, revealing the sun's rays in the delicate and lovely strands of hair. They walk barefoot through the harsh, uneven terrain. The dust adheres to their bodies and forms furrows in their skin. The most graceful movements end in murky feet that resemble severed, truncated stalks.

During the summer I never go barefoot. My brother takes some old, discarded tires and shapes them into soles. He attaches elastic bands and then we have sandals, that, apart from appearing unattractive, are sturdy and protect our feet.

I blend butter into simmering water, add some drops of alcohol and flower petals or aromatic herbs. That's how I make an ointment to soften my hands and feet. Amelia smiles and tells me that in all of the splendor of the valley there is not one plant that can match the sweet fragrance of butter when it combines with my sweat.

Doña Esmeralda finds it repulsive. She teaches me to prepare a similar lotion, but using Vaseline that she gives me. Amelia runs her fingers along my feet and hands, sniffs them and then shakes her head.

"I don't understand," she murmurs.

I'd like to explain to her how it's done. Nonetheless, I remain silent in the presence of her shadow.

Returning to Pedregal. Part of the journey we travel in a cart among sacks and burlap bags, clinging to our belongings. We travel silently, soaking in the wind. Each one is immersed in his or her own disappointment, in the loss of potential income. I'm carrying among my clothing, wrapped and hidden, the earrings and the bracelet. Quiet and pensive, I no longer hear the howling of the distant branches nor distinguish the words that, from time to time, are murmured by my brothers among the men. I need to learn how to pierce my ears and insert the earrings that defy the wind and retain the sunlight.

Don Victor gives me a blue jar with words in English, written in cursive. Inside there's a smooth, enticing cream with a penetrating and mysterious aroma. I ask him what flower is capable of such a seductive scent. He explains to me the essences, the chemistry, the extracts. I don't understand his explanations. I begin applying the cream to my face, my hands, the hollow between my breasts, and my belly; with my fingertips I spread the scented lotion all over my body. My eyes are closed and from within rich, resonant melodies flow from my mouth in a sweet song.

He then asks me to apply the cream to his naked body and I dress him with layers of cream and caresses. I don't want to waste it all on his immense body. He promises me that I'll never lack a supply of this cream if I coat his body with it now, pressing firmly and tenderly, hovering longer over the appendage that responds and throbs at the touch of my soft and perfumed fingers. After that, his skillful hands gently massage me, ascending in a circular, trembling motion; those same hands elevate my rear and deposit me with palms and knees upon the floor, my hair dangling, brushing and sweeping the ground to the sway of his tremors, gently penetrating that narrow pathway, opening it with his scented, sinuous hands until the intruder becomes comfortable in that tight space and releases so forcefully it leaves me face down on the planks of the pine floor.

I walk home in pain, my legs trembling. But my hands hold tightly to the cerulean blue jar.

In the spring, a new president will be elected in the country. Months prior to that, the candidates and those who'd like to latch onto those who win visit the towns and arrange for large parties in the town squares, in the office of the mayor, and in the clubs. Enormous trucks travel through the adjoining towns and shout out to the villagers to climb aboard, en route to San Juan. There follows an immense throng: the houses are united with garlands and flags, speakers and microphones are installed, bands arrive, and photographers seize the opportunity to capture the moment. The party members exchange glasses of wine for a commitment to vote for them. They fill buckets with wine and serve it, with unintelligible phrases pregnant with flattering words, by the ladleful to those avidly waiting to greet them, .

Villagers gush forth from hamlets like ours and finally arrive at the valley after several days of tireless trekking, despite the cold, the harsh and treacherous rocky road, and the temporary abandonment of their fields. They aren't bothered by sleeping in the open with only the stars and a cool blanket of dew in the morning to cover them

The trucks then abandon the spots where smiles have been achieved and retreat. Night falls and howls its blackness. But there's not one peasant who doesn't remain to take in the words that still float in the air.

The return home is long and arduous. The peasants are filled with promises, even if they won't go to vote or are unfamiliar with the basics of the text. The man who was given a pat on the back by a candidate is now another man, wiser, different, a fundamental part of something infinite, undefinable. As if that hand, through osmosis, had bestowed transcendence upon him and enveloped him in worldliness.

"It's all just lies and deceit," remarks Aunt Berta.

I want to go to San Juan. Six years ago during the elections, my father refused to go to the campaigns of any of the candidates. That year the only man my father could respect was abandoning his post. This time he's presenting himself for re-election. He's a distinguished gentleman with white hair and a transparent gaze. My father wants to see him and hear his speeches. When his arrival is announced, we'll all go to the valley. He's already enlisted my brothers' support, so they need to listen with the ears of adults to the voice of the man they'll elect.

The eastern wind begins to lash the land. The countryside is tinged with the crimson of turning leaves. The sky is swept by billows of whiteness. Amelia is bent forward, doing the laundry. I'm sprawled out on the chair, contemplating the colorful prism of my jewels.

The song is cheerful and melodic. As she draws near, we recognize her voice. Esther has arrived.

Pedro lives with Rosita now that she's expecting. In the beginning, he wanted to bring her here, but doña Herminia needs a man to oversee her withered tract of land. Amelia wishes there were another woman in the house. My father can't afford to lose a set of hands. Aunt Berta insists that my brother isn't obligated to get married. That if he does it just to mitigate the damage, Rosita should be grateful to him and not rob my father in that way. The sons he raised are an asset to him.

Doña Herminia argues that her land will belong to the husband of her daughter and to the children she bears with him, so Pedro should begin to work the land that will be the inheritance of his descendants.

My father finally acquiesces. He flings seed to the emaciated chickens. I tell him it's better this way, that Rosita is a woman and we women should support the decision most favorable to us.

He merely replies, "They never would have shamed me so easily." The gesture is arrogant, the voice harsh. He walks toward the house, proudly erect, with an assured stride. His hands fall trembling to the sides of his body.

Men born in arid lands, which are slow to germinate and only occasionally flourish, are not prepared for change. The cycle of life has to turn slowly and gently strip away the superficial layers. My father tells Esther to be quiet. He no longer delights in her laughter. It's no longer the refreshing breeze he longs for but rather a gale that razes and destroys.

My sister has not arrived alone. She's accompanied by a young man, Pablo. He's dressed like a peasant, but it's obvious in the fabric of the clothing he wears that it was woven and sewn by distant hands. His hair's long and he has a thick moustache that doesn't conceal his frequent and generous smile. He converses easily, the words tumbling freely, and every word uttered is the expression of the impassioned soul residing within his slender chest.

People gather around him to listen to his message, their gazes lowered. Esther raises her eyes toward him. She's silent. She only glances away when a certain phrase strikes her and unknown words run rampant inside of her. His chest pulsates rhythmically as he speaks and each syllable emitted seems like a secret invitation. Nevertheless, the men don't perceive anything extravagant, the women aren't mistrustful of his opulence, nor are young girls enthralled by his smooth skin. That's how powerful his words are.

Don Victor has a son. His wife died in childbirth. They say that he resented that little piece of life that had the strength to destroy the life of another. He left the child, still cooing in the cradle, and took off. Rumor has it that he was in the valley and through schemes amassed a small fortune. Every summer he returned. He resolved to make the land more productive, bringing machines and seeds. Within the confines of his home, he observed the progress of his son. Manuel was dark and lanky, totally unlike his father. They raised him to be weak and timid, a reflection of the fear of his Aunt Erna, who'd achieved the unforeseen social prominence upon which the survival of the child depended.

Don Victor went on to purchase half a block in the town and built the first store in Pedregal with four different departments and a cash register. The villagers used to gather outside the store just to hear the ringing of the machine as it opened and closed. He placed his sister, Erna, in charge and took his son to the valley. Unlike her brother, doña Erna was a disaster with finances. The store was entrusted to a manager sent by don Victor and the woman began to drink heavily. They say she blames her downfall on the fact that the child was taken from her—especially when they moved him to the capital and she could no longer be near him.

Aunt Berta says she was always a lost cause, that she never married because she no longer had any mystery to reveal to a man, that the abyss of alcohol was a pale reflection of the punishment that awaited her, and losing the child was what she deserved for all those children she shamelessly rejected and never carried in her womb.

No one knows why don Victor returned. It happened gradually and silently, as if enchantment subtly emanated from the land and penetrated his dreams.

Winter was slipping away, the earth changing color and opening the first chasms. A child ran to the top of the hill that dominates the path. He stood there for hours wrestling with the wind, his gaze fixed upon the dusty and empty remnant of land.

Amelia only remembers that image of him.

"He was waiting for the older gentleman," Esther remarks.

One of those afternoons I unwrap my jewels from among the cloth and copper. Pablo has gone to Sauzal to scatter his words. Esther clears the air, singing with a voice the wind can't pierce, a voice that hasn't absorbed the aridness of the air and whose melody banishes the accumulating dust.

I approach her with my hands in fists. My nails are trimmed but they still dig into my palms. I slowly release the pressure in my hands and there appears the brilliance of the gems and metals.

"It's a secret," I tell her.

She's not the least bit dazzled, not even for an instant. She explains to me that they're simply cheap baubles, gold-colored wire that is wound with pieces of glass in a tawdry setting.

"Where did you get those?" Her question shakes the entire core of my being, but the tone is so casual that I quickly recover and respond that I bought them in El Paso.

She encourages me to wear them. She heats a needle in the fire and pierces my ears. The pain is brief, somewhat sharp. But I can't stop feeling the soft swaying of the earrings. The bracelet interferes with my tasks, with each movement sweetly distracting me.

I know that Esther, in the depths of her being, is laughing at what she perceives as a harmless vanity. I'm fine with that, as long as she's willing to say that she gave me the jewelry. Her reply: "Of course, though I would have given you more beautiful jewels."

The sun becomes crimson. I cover it with the largest of the rubies. The colors fuse together and then separate, scattering sparkles up my arm.

"They're not cheap baubles," I tell her.

Pablo tells us that men are gathering in the cities. That the new movement has excited people. That this year centuries of oppression will be overthrown by a new social order. He removes an apparatus unfamiliar to us from his bag and inserts a tape. An insurmountable song overflows with the voices of men and women who are struggling for freedom. Their forceful expression lights the night and heads are held high with an impetus none of us have known. Eyes shine, glowing with the reflection of the promises suspended in the air. Slowly, hesitant voices harmonize and join in the singing. In a matter of days, there's more spirit in these voices than in the chorus coming from the recording machine.

My father prohibits the music and speeches on his land. His voice withers in the solitary evenings. I accompany him. I tell Amelia which pasture the young men will be gathering in this time. She replies that she's not going to go against the wishes of her father, that my brothers, poisoned by the lies of Pablo and Esther, can rush off to hear him.

Aunt Berta approaches when the moon is full. She tells us where they are and what they've said.

"Be quiet," my father tells her, as if by not speaking the truth, the deeds could be mitigated. She wasn't born to be silent and explains the dangers inherent in a desire to attempt to change the natural order that's been placed upon us.

Esther tells me that the finer things are no longer important and that privileges are going to disappear. No longer will the wealthy man be envied, but rather rejected. When souls have become whole again and they embrace this way of thinking, then jewels and finery will no longer be produced as they only corrupt individuals in their pursuit to possess them.

She confesses to me that it's somewhat difficult to dismiss vanity, but that the companions on this journey aren't attracted to women adorned with jewels. Upon discarding these adornments, men can see a woman in all her humanity and not through layers of appearances and stereotypes. Finally men and women will walk together hand in hand, without one in front of the other. The liberation of the oppressed will extend into families, schools, factories, and the countryside.

My father's right: Esther's changed. What she was unable to achieve in the stifling confines of her childhood, she's attained with a handful of reiterated words.

The little girl strolls through the countryside. The valley that she crosses is verdant and full of flowers. Her dress is white, made with many layers of sheer silk fabric which ripple in the wind, becoming separate and then recombined in a new way. Her long blonde hair, freely swaying in time, captures the sun's rays and fuses with them, resulting in radiant shades. With her hand, she adjusts the straw hat on her head, the ribbons accompanying the rhythm of her stride. She doesn't wear jewels, just earrings in all their splendor. She traverses the hill and then descends into a hollow. Her steps are tiny, but each movement is elongated and enveloping.

She descends to the black circular hole where the water forms a pool. The breeze has lifted and the pond is a terse, luminous mirror. Even without silver or glass, it seems to shatter thunderously upon flinging into the water my dark and tired figure.

Esther leaves one morning. She takes the few things she brought with her. Pablo carries his own belongings and the tape recording machine.

Work is busy at this time in the fields, but a growing number of men and women accompany them to the curve in the path. At the beginning, it's a slow and silent procession. Soon, a voice begins singing the song which has overcome their souls, and then all the voices harmonize and the song cascades over the marchers. It's an impetuous tone. Swift and muffled, the steps of the people traverse the various curves of the rocky road. Alone on the forking path, Pablo dismisses them. He reminds them of their promises to organize and emphasizes to the peasants that they've made this grand project their own. He urges them to exert themselves, to not be afraid to approach groups that are forming in other nearby towns. They'll return soon and they've put their trust in the people, in the advances that will be made during these coming weeks.

"Now is the time," he insists. That's what he most repeats. It enters my veins and runs through my entire body. I don't have any idea what he's referring to. The *now* is already here, palpitating in every one of us. I don't know what the *now* of others is, nor the *now* that's mine.

Some nights the moon creeps into my bed and flings the blanket to the floor. Then it slides up to my eyes and draws back my eyelids. The night's clear and I can see the silhouette of my mother. She inclines, stands up, moves her hands diligently in endless activity. She doesn't move from that place, as if she fit only into that spot on earth and should be content to remain there.

I can't see her face. I cover my eyes with my hands and arms. I tremble. I don't shake the image of her face until daybreak.

A light rain falls. It adheres to the dust that covers our clothing and slides away. Slow and silent is the muddy stride of my father. All around us, the autumn wind with its wicked jabs.

My sister's going to register to vote. There's no registration office in the village, merely a young man appointed for the position, installed in don Victor's store. From a stool that doesn't even reach the countertop, he extends a large notebook. Amelia signs unhurriedly, her face almost touching the page. The young man looks at her and drums his fingers on top of the wooden counter. Others are waiting their turn. With a disparaging look, the official glances at them. Amelia's face is full of color and even with her hair pulled back tightly, several locks fall over her forehead. My father fidgets with his hat. Time seems to stand still within the store. I remove a couple coins from my pocket and they fall to the floor. They roll ever so slowly, tracing lines as they travel in their eternal track. Amelia clings to the pencil and the coins continue, endlessly, to roll.

This is what the women say. But not to me. It's what they gossip about among themselves—a skein in which there is no idle hand:

Manuel has arrived in Pedregal. Two youths accompany him. They very much resemble Pablo. From their mouths flow the same enchanting words. The only difference is that they don't do this under the stars nor do they speak among the hills. They perch themselves up high and speak with determined looks on their faces. They travel through the countryside, summoning men and women. They don't implore. They hold meetings filled with such tenderness and command that even the most timid, barely-insinuated statements emerge with force. Thick roots rip chests and bellies from the earth. Entangled branches urgently bud, and from each bud a flower blossoms. A moveable forest gathers, intertwines, loosens, and knits an invisible network of hope.

Rumor from all the cardinal points has it that don Victor won't hear of this in his house. That Manuel hasn't knocked on his closed door. That he's crossed dusty thresholds where other doors opened at the sound of his steps. That at so many tables there's a place set for him. That from every oven there's always the whitest, most worthy bread—the greatest offering and the most simple.

On land that will one day be Pedro's, a wooden shack is constructed in just a matter of days. They gather there in the afternoons and let go of their fatigue to clear space for the weariness that will accompany them on this new journey.

Doña Herminia toils at her tasks next to the window. She doesn't say a word until the rain falls and rain-soaked women run across her land. Then she emits a sound from deep inside and runs through the hills. Many are the hours she spends in the shack, coming and going, diligently traveling roads mud has eroded to reach more women. She fills her hands, and little by little, she empties them.

We don't go to San Juan. My father's candidate appeared in these parts. But now the other candidate's entourage, indeed, has come. Esther ar-

40

rives. With a single gesture she forms a caravan. They depart cheerfully and the air here is heavy. The dome of the sky narrows and turns gray, enveloping us on this empty ridge.

My brothers go with them. Rosa and their newborn child stay with us. My father has aged. Few new wrinkles appear in his skin, but every day those already there seem to become more profound and extensive. His body becomes more shriveled. He's just one more seed that never blossomed.

Rain seeps through cracks. The walls are damp and I draw close to them, first facing them then turning my back and sides to them. My clothing is soaked, and through my skin I absorb the water. It moves through me. I can't contain it, I don't know what it is nor how to remove it.

Don Victor tells me he's going to vote for the senseless one, the one that has promised the impossible. And when the party's over and the hangover brings disenchantment, he won't have to listen to people scream about their unproductive land. The valleys will no longer be parceled out and distributed to the hands of incompetent peasants. One oligarchy will be dethroned to create a new one without the power of inheritance or the destruction of order that brutal oligarchies need.

I don't understand his words. Nor those of the others. But don Victor's words are harsh and embittered, they assault and darken the gazes of the peasants. As long as they subvert their desire for land and make the land productive, they possess the sweet impetus of the wind.

The rumor about the victory spreads like a river overflowing its banks, a cadenced and constant sound that splits open in an instant, creating an avalanche of water and stones that strikes, heaves, shoves its load toward what's static, shaking the banks, penetrating layers until it reaches the innermost secrets guarded by the earth. The torrent inundates and then retreats, an inescapable tide that carries entire families to San Juan. Improvised flags that are coarsely woven wave among the heads, and such is the force produced by the throng that the land, giving way to the initial upsurge, appears to be covered by the tenuous mantle of a dark springtime.

The bride's dress has been soiled by the sides of the wheels. A tan stripe stains the white dress. The ceremony is swift and the party interminable. Airy intertwined branches rustle in a nocturnal reverence. Animals roast on spits over open fires. Wine flows freely. The moon hovers over the bride's dress. Some insects become entangled in the folds of her skirt. The bouquet, covered with dust, inclines wearily toward the hand in which it withers.

I run from my hiding place to the house. I tell Amelia what I've seen, but I don't speak about the sparkle that emanated from the bride's body or the uncontainable brightness in the eyes of Jose.

The commotion last night that sundered the darkness suppresses my words. She'd lain down facing the wall, her crying soft and silent as a wounded bird in the hollow of one's hands.

Aunt Bertha lives with her daughter, Ana. As if she had intuited her face, she baptized her with that name. Small and scrawny, her mousy features are miserly in her insignificant face. Ana. It rhymes with nothing. Nevertheless, from the matrix opened in her thighs, every year she gives birth to a healthy, robust child that screams with the force of one who fears getting lost in the silence of the mist. Dispersed around the house, they seem like the pickets of a fence.

Ana is about to give birth. Aunt Bertha's hands have agilely handled the slippery entrance of many children into this world. She knows how to skillfully introduce her arm into the dense tunnel of women and with a precise movement twists the covering with which nature dresses and covers itself. This time she asks Amelia to accompany her. She doesn't want to become a renowned midwife because that's the profession of an old maid, butshe agrees to go along. I follow closely behind carrying items that are neeeded. I tell her I want to help, even though my true interest is in seeing the harsh flowering of the womb.

They leave me outside, in charge of the children in the quagmire. I count them and forget how many. Their game is to chase me. Slight shadows run around the hills and become entangled in the thickets, among which I spot Manuel. He's sitting erect on the slope, and even though he has an open notebook on his lap, his gaze wanders among the hills. I retreat and join the children. Manuel sees us and smiles. I say to him, "I thought you'd gone away."

He responds in the negative, telling me that now more than ever it's imperative to organize against climate change. I don't understand why. Nothing seismic is hovering over the rocky terrain. He explains to me that change is not immediate and that pebbles and stones fortify walls. The sandy surf laps the shore is but is part of an immense wave that will erupt and crash.

I tell him I've never seen the sea. He proceeds to remove a piece of paper from his notebook and spills upon it a torrent of ink by squeezing the cartridge inside his pen. He takes the two sides of the paper with both hands and makes the ink oscillate until it dries. He shows us a dark stain resembling a spider. On the extremity of one of those legs, brushing the last hair, there we are. On other points, there are other towns, more distant, other droughts. Regardless of remoteness and distance, all are connected to the vibrations of the body. Water may arrive slowly, haltingly, but it will flood the arid land until it erases all traces of men.

The stained piece of paper passes among the children's hands. Manuel takes out others. Into each one, he spills a little ink until the pen dries up. The children laugh. They try to guess the meaning of the figures on the paper. Their dark fingers caress the white borders. We say our goodbyes and descend. Passion and tenderness among the thickets. I don't know what else I'm leaving behind. The newborn cries in the house. The smell is nauseating. I refuse to enter. I remain in the doorway, blocking the wind.

I hide the inkblot under my bed. I try to understand the words I remember. I can't. Amelia thinks Manuel's a dreamer. She says, without emotion, "He's far from what one would expect."

My brothers admire him. Other young men do as well. I listen to what they say about him. It seems that everyone is moved when they see him perched up high. But what they most admire is his demeanor, which has been bestowed upon him by events and fate.

Not me. Men rise and above their heads are the bellies of other men. Each height is surpassed. I'd love to revel in their dreams, bathe in the ocean of their convictions. Mount and ride the beast of their expectations, and then watch them fall from the heights into the gnarl of torment, the apex of their conviction turned to dust.

Summer. Fairs, farmer's markets, excursions. Pretexts that all lead to the valley. They imagine it fragmented. Green cloths embroidered with their monograms. Roads that wind and splinter into others. Labyrinth that blossoms beyond the next bend. Bags draped over their backs. Dragging their poverty behind them. Faces and footsteps turned toward the east. The wind is ambivalent. It no longer blows in the right direction. It swirls helplessly. It stirs up dust that hasn't even settled. The bleeting of sheep severs the sunset. Shoddily-trimmed pine trees entangle their wool. Nostrils askance attempting to draw the curtains, the thick dark vegetation revealing obscure passages that lead to an empty murkiness. And there we are wherever, indiscriminately.

I pass by don Victor's house. For months the windows have been closed. The surrounding garden is overrun with weeds. Some afternoons the silhouette of doña Ermina is visible. They say that most of the time she's tumbled over and clutching a bottle. That's not true. At times she totters among the hills. She steadies herself by grabbing onto a tree. The tree's bark leaves an indelible imprint upon her face. The tears she sheds among the trees slip swiftly away, muddled with the rain.

With the chillier winds, those who'd left return. They depart again, taking women and children they'd left behind with them. They speak about the others, those who have yet to traverse the extensive land. Few remain, only the owners of the land. It's just a few.

My father has lost the hands of his sons. Hunched over his tasks, he sees the slow yet inexorable march of the weeds overtaking the land where he spent his youth. Silence has swallowed him. Amelia no longer sings in a hushed voice. He swats the puppies. The animals eat silently. The pines appease the shrill wind. I run beneath the rain. My white dress is tattered. Amelia scrubs the tattered pieces of cloth that remain. I cover myself with the woolen blanket that was my mother's. I can barely hear the splashing of my feet in the puddles.

What's left?

Me.

Amelia.

Shadows on Amelia's face.

Aunt Bertha.

Ana and Rosa.

Some children.

My father.

The weariness of my father.

Families torn apart.

The opacity of my jewels.

An empty blue container.

The deserted road.

The burlap from some sacks.

A meager harvest.

Mice among the grain.
Minutes and hours of silence.
The curve of the horizon.
A cemetery that appears in a dream.
Fissures throughout the arid land.
Clouded eyes.
Dust in the clouds.
Lowered eyes.

We've lowered our eyes because we didn't stand up and turn toward the east like those others did.

Spring's ending, I let go of my skeins of wool. I no longer have a dress. Amelia is thinking about fixing my mother's flowered dress for me but I don't want that print on my body. My mother never came out from under that fabric. She was always tethered to it. I'm fearful of that frenetic movement, like a drill upon the land, stationary, spinning, digging an endless hole, always darker and more narrow.

Amelia modifies it to fit her. She mends for me a dress that belonged to Esther and has lost its color with use and time. In our scraps of cloth, we trudge to church. I don't have a veil, so my hair's exposed. The benches don't have backs. Few are the men hunched toward the altar. The shadows of midday sway without melding. Father Benito's voice is tremorous. A song about damp terrain that's creating the muddy swamp into which all our stones, one by one, are sinking.

The sun's already high overhead the morning Esther appears. She's wearing a short skirt. My father tells her to cover herself. She feigns a sigh and slips on Amelia's worn sweater. Her skin's tanned and she often smiles while her fingers fidget with a medallion.

"I thought you no longer wore jewelry," I say to her.

She explains to me that it's not an adornment, but rather a symbol, something that reflects to others her feelings and her determination to not deviate from the journey. I don't understand the difference and she doesn't rush to flood me with clarification.

She talks about a large tract of land in the valley that belonged to just one family, millions of acres scarcely cultivated, immense parcels abandoned to future generations. While the peasants filled the granaries with their ceaseless labor, their own homes were overflowing with misery, ignorance and humiliation. Now, however, the situation is reversed and the peasants have become the owners of the very land that, for generations, they worked tirelessly. There will no longer be landowners who can't see the limits of their property. Nor are fields left fallow, because we should caress, not crush, the hand that feeds all of us.

She continues to explain that on those large estates, there are enormous and lofty houses, surrounded by covered paths and parks with such a variety of plants that throughout the year there's always an abundance of green and color. Today more than twenty families reside in just one of those mansions, with a spaciousness they never knew.

My father murmurs something about the time in which he became the owner of his land. Of how he paid dearly for years for the price of the parcel. Of the countless privations endured to leave his sons an inheritance. Of the numerous nights he fell asleep while praying to the heavens for more rain.

"You people are stealing," he concludes, with a voice that has almost become inaudible.

Esther insists that the fruits of the land can no longer be subjected to the whims of an owner, that nature knows no bounds, that rivers don't hoard their water.

But my father identifies more with the dispossessed and upon ending the discussion he states that, no matter what, it would be unjust if he were stripped of his land or his sons robbed of their inheritance.

Esther laughs. She hugs her father and tells him to relax because nobody would be interested in the redistribution of his land.

"And why not?" I ask. I know her answer, but my father's uneasiness makes me ask.

"Because we're talking about fertile land, not…this." Her disparaging gesture toward the surroundings causes my father to stand up. His hands are trembling as he forces her out of the house.

School's over for me. There's no ceremony. They give me a certificate with two stamps and four signatures. The grades are written in blue ink and the ornate penmanship of the director. The venerable document is covered by a blank sheet of paper. A somewhat rusty paper clip holds them together.

They dismiss me with an embrace. Without tenderness or pride. I hadn't even turned toward the door when all traces of me were erased.

The teachers have arranged for two of the girls in my class to go to San Juan to continue studying to become, like them, rural schoolteachers. Four or so are going to finish eighth grade and then attend a technical school. The rest of us are to spill out into the countryside and become good wives and mothers. The more ambitious ones will move to a small city and find a home where they can work as domestic help. It's possible that one might even enter the convent or a house of prostitution.

I take all the used notebooks. Mine and those of my classmates. All that I can carry. They look at me strangely. Just for a moment. In a flash, I fade from all memory.

Aunt Bertha talks as we spin the wool onto the spindle. She always asks herself what sin my mother committed to deserve Esther. If there's no apparent failing, then it was because of impure thoughts. My silence serves to fuel her discussion. She speaks about hearts in which discontent resides, of how false pride results in a sense of entitlement of the most lofty design and contempt for those who work the solemn way of the Lord.

My fingers advance more swiftly than hers, as if in this task I could release the dead weight which, like a pendulum, sways in the vacuum that has installed itself inside of me.

Esther stays at Pablo's house. I'm going to see her before she leaves. She's in charge of a small agrarian community, preparing women to work cooperatively and guiding them in the upbringing of their children. Pablo works in the cellar of a storage building in the community with which Esther is involved. He occupies a position of prominence and soon will be promoted, as his commitment to the movement is clear to all, and she won't diminish him in the eyes of others.

Esther now seems more like herself: a whimsical, smiling young girl. Only now her whims are enveloped in layers of deception and blindly tugged to the limit of all she's plowed.

Ana leans over to pick up the child to breastfeed him. He's still warm, and delicate. Cerulean pathways with no apparent direction mark his face and hands.

The mother's scream shatters the silence of the afternoon. Arrhythmic cries arise from the other children. The absolute silence that follows the laments is worse. Words are useless against the relentless glare of the sun upon that small body, now wrapped in cloths that were his diapers.

The wake that goes into the night is stifling. Ana cries because he hadn't been baptized and Father Benito is sick. Nobody is going to assist the little angel in his ascent to the pastures of the Lord.

Aunt Bertha recites passages from Psalms. Ana's father-in-law painfully reads a prayer. Dawn is hushed in the hollows of the cemetery. Warm shadows hover over the grave. Only loose dirt wraps its arms around the child.

When the others have retreated, I run home. I return with the veil from my First Communion and let it fall upon the small mound.

After the burial, Esther leaves. I walk with her for some of the way. I want to talk to her, but I don't find words that will draw us closer, so we walk mostly in silence. At times, she's chatty, but there's nothing I can add. Esther doesn't seem aware of this new distance.

Abruptly I ask about Manuel. It's been awhile since she's seen him. They proposed that he take charge of the mill, of the agrarian society, of the distribution of cereals, or of the slaughterhouse.

"All fabulous positions," she says, without hiding her admiration and desire for him to take on those posts.

But Manuel refused to accept them. He prefers to lose himself in the more distant countryside organizing literacy groups, self-help groups, and laying the foundations for agriculture and livestock. He's stooped to the lowest, most sluggish, and least productive of the struggles.

"Having so many other opportunities! I don't understand," she sighs. I don't understand either. Regardless, what Esther shares with me lightens my steps. The hollowness inside no longer feels heavy, as if just the knowledge of Manuel's faith has the strength to exalt the wind.

Amelia helps my father. I help Amelia around the house. I also head out to the fields. I knit. Wherever I may be, I always carry a notebook beneath my blouse and a pencil that I sharpen with a knife. Whenever I can, I slip away and scribble numbers. I add and subtract them. An interminable ladder of figures that always ends the same. More rapidly. Even longer is the snail that slithers around the borders of the pages. When I can calculate in my mind each column without resorting to counting on my fingers or taking notes in the margins, I begin to multiply and divide.

The withered leaves of autumn begin to fall upon the scorned earth. I ponder the numbers in their totality.

The clouds and sky appear dressed in mourning this morning. The air is still. Gray. Sharp pricks penetrate my skin. Some birds fly from one tree to another. I slowly advance along the only road I know. My legs move with the utmost agility. Birds swarm about incessantly. They change direction, purpose, and velocity so rapidly that the earth seems like the muddy bank of an endless river.

Don Victor's store still is closed. I wait patiently, leaning against the door. The man in charge unlocks from inside and opens the door. The light that strikes him doesn't affect his drowsiness. I wait for him to open the curtains, remove the cover from the cash register, lay paper upon the counter, and place a pencil behind his ear.

I approach the casks. With the tip of my finger I trace the edge of the circular piece of wood. I ask him if he knows where don Victor is and why he hasn't returned for such a long time. He grudgingly tells me that he now lives in San Juan, where he has land and businesses. He doubts that he'll return.

"To what?" he concludes.

I hand him an envelope with a letter. I beg him to be sure that he receives it. He shrugs his shoulders and tells me that he'll include it along with other corresondence next week. I thank him and leave. On the loamy land, I begin to wait. Now to wait.

On the nights when there's a full moon, the clarity thrashes my face. Next to me, against the wall, Amelia is in restless sleep. At our feet, at a right angle, my father sleeps without moving. Different sounds emerge from his chest. Near the corner is the stove filled with ashes. The table has warped, as has the wood of the two stands upon which trinkets are balanced. Clothing and blankets hang from hooks on the walls. The earth's rough soil makes tenuous shadows undulate. The center of the room is empty. I sit on the dilapidated bed awaiting the specter of my mother. I tremble. I'm not sure it's because of the wind that seeps into every pore of my body. Night advances. It weighs on my eyelids. I eventually fall asleep. She doesn't come.

The landscape at midday, between morning and evening, opens its broad, black mouth and swallows up the dry dust. Thick clouds have unraveled. A crimson sun extends its arms in a long yawn, awakens over the devastated land, and rolls across decay and buds that never blossomed. The weight of the heat makes the fissures in the ground even more pronounced. The wind retreats, but the scorched air caresses my shoulders, slapping them until I'm hunched over, defeated by the inexhaustible drought.

My letter consists of gray strokes that brush along the greenish page of a notebook with equally greenish lines. Hands, small and thick, move across paper that screams, implores, humbles itself, and allows itself to be wrinkled up and tossed to the farthest corner. The dirt begs with all its silence for a gesture, any gesture.

Another summer without going to El Paso.

How can nights repeat themselves without daylight?

My father is accompanied by Pedro. They'll return soon, the empty burlap bags even emptier than before.

Once again Rosa is expecting. Amelia helps her with her son. Every evening the women gather to knit, mend, corral the animals, knead the bread, and prepare meals. They barely speak. The young boy is growing up shrouded in silence. He sits on the floor smashing stones. He places them in a jar and then disperses them again. He clutches one of them and puts it in his mouth, which becomes smeared with saliva and dust. Innumerable times he's tasted the arid savor of his land, as if he were never going to know another.

Aunt Bertha comes around occasionally in the evenings, some work spreading through her hands. She always finds a way to give a detailed report about the behavior of doña Herminia, a woman who neglects her essential duties to spend hours in irrefutable, morally questionable groups, fighting for something as intangible as smoke. There must be some purpose, something hidden that, for minds like doña Herminia's, it's difficult to imagine. Perhaps that's due to her penchant for intermingling with others who, like her, waste their time searching for a pretext to discover themselves and who speak about what doesn't exist. Surrounded, of course, by young men wrapped up in words and leisure and, although they don't recognize it, that inevitable force, the inexhaustible thirst that is satiated in whatever fountain is nearest and most accessible. For those who permit that chaos to reign, it's as if they were emptying a basket of snakes. They're simply sowing on this earth that most wicked of weeds, the one thing that's nurtured in the soul of an individual.

Rosa hears her speak. She opens her eyes wide. There's no fear in those eyes, no indignation nor surprise. It's an intensely ignorant, imperceptive gaze.

Amelia doesn't say a word. In the beginning. Then slowly, she begins to agree and mumble words of complacency. I leave. The first winds of autumn are arriving. I don't receive any letters. Not one.

One afternoon he arrives. Upon opening the door, his footsteps make the wooden floor resound. Amelia and I are piling the dirty dishes to take them outside to the washtub we've prepared. Our father is seated. He stands up upon seeing him. His body appears much scrawnier next to the portliness of don Victor. It's as if the entire room is going to collapse under his presence. The discord is disconcerting and we're immobilized. Three mouths wide open. Six eyes that don't blink. Two arms that literally drop to the side and the noisy shattering of dishes as they fall silently to the floor.

Don Victor has come to take me. He tells my father that he needs an employee in his business and since I'm honest and skilled with numbers, not to mention young enough to learn the trade to his satisfaction, he'd be most grateful if my father allowed him to take me to the city of San Juan under his protection. And fully aware of the reaction that could be provoked, he adds that they're both from the same land and that should suffice. He offers a payment that he'll send almost entirely to my father, so he can help out with what's needed on my father's parcels of land. He tells my father there's a room in the back of the store, and that I'm going to have a roof over my head and food and no opportunity to go out and have a good time, that he would kindly repay the confidence bestowed upon him.

My father remains standing, silent. With a gesture of his hand, he tells Amelia and me to leave. Moments later we see don Victor departing. I learn that my father has accepted this work for me. Leaning against the doorway, I watch him walk away without looking back.

The night draws me through a labyrinth of dreams. I am see myself confused with the images of a green valley over which a bright, burnished sun bursts with a sweet and dense essence; a long table, whose end is not visible, rises and descends. I jump upon it and dance in high heels which resound along it with the applause of the others. And then Aunt Bertha arrives

51

and strikes the table, which begins to rise and become smaller; I can no longer keep my balance in my high heels; a curtain appears that I can't close, time advances and I'm no longer able to close the curtain. I take planks from a dresser and hammer them into the window, but they don't reach, and they're coming because they know I can no longer close the curtains. My mother enters and doesn't recognize me. She asks me for a package of sugar, and she doesn't have enough to pay for it. She asks me for a smaller package and again she can't pay for it. The bundle of money is so slim it slides through my fingers, but she continues, despite not having the appropriate amount of money. I tell her not to worry, that she can take the package with her without paying, and I begin to search for it on the floor and each time I find it, it slips through my fingers, and my mother tells me not to worry, and I want to run after her, but I can't find the end of the table, and I run from one end to the other while I watch her walk away.

Why me?

Where did don Victor get the idea that I had a knack for numbers?

Why take an ignorant girl to a city filled with competent individuals?

How is it that a man of his position should be concerned about my father, with whom he has never spoken?

Is it possible that nobody bothered to ask what other intentions might be hidden in this overture?

How certain is it that he'll fulfill his promises?

Can he be confident that I'll be capable of responding to his demands, if to date I've never demonstrated such a capacity?

Who says honest people are born here, given that, for no reason, we're divided?

What is he thinking when he believes that because I'm younger, that I won't have my idiosyncrasies?

Theses are Aunt Bertha's questions. The sight of my dusky, barren body prevents her from offering the answers that writhe inside of her.

Amelia accompanies me to El Paso. I don't have either a bag or a basket. Nor anything to throw inside. I carry my belongings wrapped in a blanket that we've secured with a strip of wool. Aunt Berta insists that one of her sons-in-law obtains a cart to ease the burden of the journey. We settle ourselves on top of the bags. She also climbs aboard. She's not about to allow Amelia to return alone in the company of the young men. The pil-

grimage is long. The bumps in the rocky road and my aunt's recommenda-
tions put me to sleep, her incessant, disorderly warnings about temptations
that, if not rejected in time, could cause me to behave in an unbecoming
way along arid and slippery slopes.

Twice a week the bus leaves the town and travels to San Juan. Even
though it's overcast, it's still stifling hot. I find a seat next to a window with
cracked glass. Amelia and Aunt Berta accompany me until the driver turns
on the motor. The entire vehicle shakes and tickles our feet. The three of us
are amused. We grab on tightly to the iron rails. The driver shouts: "We're
leaving! Get off the bus if you don't have a ticket!" I stand up, frightened by
the tone of his voice. Aunt Bertha gives me a shove and I fall back into my
seat.

"It's you who's traveling," she tells me.

Once again, I'm overcome with laughter, as are the two of them. We
say goodbye with a smile. They look so small from the height of the window.
My arm grows weary from so much waving. The bus begins to move and I
no longer see them. Traveling next to me is a heavy-set man reading the newspaper. He spreads open the pages of the newspaper, and I have to retreat to
the far side. I enjoy studying the landscape. Suddenly, I realize that the three
of us had never laughed out loud together before.

The road is winding. The speed of the bus changes brusquely with
each curve. I'm dizzy and light-headed. I cut off small pieces of bread, but
it's difficult for me to swallow them. I feel like I might vomit. The window
won't open. The nausea mixes with the anguish of not knowing where to
spew the bile that lurches in my throat nor how to get out of my seat if the
gentleman next to me is sleeping and his protruding stomach impedes my
passage. The glass flattens my cheek. I squeeze my bundled belongings tightly,
so tightly I can no longer endure it. My eyes tear up and a salty taste is fused
with the bitterness in my mouth. The bus slides along the descending curves.

I close my eyes and he appears. His lands extend like overflowing
water. The crops have been harvested recently and I can still see green pastures in which cattle and horses graze freely, unhurriedly, choosing the most
tender blades among the grass. Swathes of fallow land that will feel soft and
still to the touch of the plow. On both sides of the road, poplars capture
handfuls of sunlight in their leaves and toy with them as if they were kites
in springtime.

The bus advances indifferently among a landscape of unending variety. I can't form an image when it's overcome by another and another and another.

Different vehicles pass one another or overtake us and we provide a breeze to the cyclists and the horseback riders advancing along the side of the road.

The bus slows. We're momentarily detained. We take off once again. Another standstill. The passengers get off the bus and head in every direction. I see the first houses, followed by a row of doors, windows, signs, people heading in every direction, a noisy din of bustling in which sounds are inseparable,

"Get to the plaza," my father told me. His words resound inside me as, clutching my belongings, I exit the bus.

The plaza of Pedregal is nothing more than an irregular space in front of a church where several rocks are stacked to resemble seats and there are a couple of tired trees, beneath which are some disintegrating wooden benches.

In San Juan, among asphalt streets, avenues and various construction projects, there sits an enormous plaza. The entire perimeter is surrounded by colorful flowers, and out of these emerge narrow and level walkways that converge in the interior, where a white gazebo, with walls made of crisscrossing wooden slats and two circular balconies, stands. On each side of the gazebo are two poles with flags at the top. The wind passes gently without disturbing the gazebo's dome. Each tree is distinct from the previous one and their crowns project hulking shadows. Several benches of white, intricately-forged iron appear to open themselves in a silent invitation. In each quadrant of the soft dirt, upon white stone pedestals, monuments to patriots of the country who were born in San Juan have been erected. The lampposts are intertwined with garlands of lights, as if they wanted to enshrine and remember all the beauty of this plaza.

Upon alighting on the pavement, the tolling of the church's lofty bells begins. The open tower reveals them. Three gleaming bells swaying in the heavens. The sun surely is about to set far away, on the sea. Above the rooftops, crimson brushstrokes dismiss the afternoon. A murmur accompanies the steps of the people that pass by me. Nobody sees my wide eyes in the corner of the plaza.

Don Victor appears behind me. He says, "And your things?"

I show him the bundle, which has begun to become undone.

54

"Just that? All right . . .." With an abrupt gesture, he takes me by the elbow and we cross the street. He loosens his grip and walks alone. His strides are long and fast. I run after him in a trot and still can't reach him. Besides, I have to wipe away the tears that surface. "Just that?" Yes, that's all I have, my few things and those Amelia gave me, things that were hers, my mother's, or Esther's discards.

I remember doña Esmeralda. Months have passed without me recalling her. She insisted I go with her that summer, that afterward it would be too late, that I was only going to be desirable while my body was fragile and my cheeks smooth, that as soon as a man considered me damaged goods he wouldn't pay a cent for me, that the widening of my hips would be the definitive misfortune, that men fantasize about virgins, desiring to stretch them open with their hands until they're satisfied and overflow in their fingers.

I'm still small and scrawny. The flesh clings to my bones and my skin shimmers when it comes into contact with water. But the dullness of my eyes reveals that the winters are adding up.

The store's a few blocks from the plaza. It occupies almost the length of the street between one corner and another. A green sign crowns it. On each outside end there's a blackboard where it's written what there is and what there isn't.

The curtains are drawn. In the dimness I see that the shelves are all empty. Behind an angle of the counter is an open door. The hallway's wide. Several doors are visible in the adobe walls. All of them have large locks.

"They're wine cellars," explains don Victor. He places a hand on my waist, and with his free hand he turns the key in the lock of the last door.

The room's spacious. It doesn't have a window. On one of the walls an enormous wardrobe is placed next to an oval mirror. At the foot of the bed, a curtain. He pulls it aside and shows me that it's a bathroom and how the translucent water flows and never ceases. And the toilet. I want to know where all that filth goes. I'm not capable of imagining all he's explaining to me. Pipes that bring clean water and carry that which has already been used away to the point at which it no longer smells foul.

He tells me to try it. I'm so accustomed to emptying my bladder while squatting that it takes me a while to begin the flow over the mirror of water upon which I'm seated. The relief becomes pleasure that ascends warmly. He offers to show me how he uses it.

"Don't get up," he says.

He forces my legs open until a triangular space appears. Down comes flowing a thick, sonorous stream of water that, at times, sprays my legs, lashing them with the blazing blades of a thousand knives while my hands freeze, hugging tightly the porcelain basin.

He teaches me to use the shower. I shiver beneath the stream of water. He then enters. He pushes my face against the tiles. From behind he enters me. The weight of his body and the noise of the water muffle screams I'm unable to contain.

I arise early, when the first sounds are still sleeping and don't come near the walls of my room, when the labyrinth of the streets is still shrouded in silence.

I enter the bathroom with a lighted candle. I'm not accustomed to the harshness of the bulb that hangs from the ceiling. Under the freezing water, I cover every part of my body with the soap's lather. I shut off the water and remain standing, combing my hair until it becomes strands. Then I turn the water back on, and it slides along the whiteness covering me. I caress my body with talcum powder, cream and lotion—all that don Victor has brought me. Stretched out on the bed, without clothing, I doze off to sleep awaiting the clamor of the streets.

The store opens as soon as the sky becomes light. There are several departments. The majority are empty. Don Victor explains that it's because of the trucks, because they're not working in the factories, because they've cut off some road, because, in short, the government is worthless. The customers lean on the counter to complain and end up taking home something. They pay with cash. Several bills are the equivalent of cents. They don't fit in the women's coin purses and are too bulky for the pockets of the men.

Don Victor put three tables with chairs in the store. He offers drinks of whatever there is, slices of *roulade, pebre* and *pan amasado*. I wait on the persons who sit to rest a moment but stay for a long while repeating something they've heard. I hear so many rumors, so varied and contrary, that at the end of the day, they're all tangled together in my head. I begin to not hear them. Some of them. The voice of don Victor repeats what they've told him. According to whom he listens, he speaks in a serious or joking or angry tone. The people stand around the tables, exchanging bills for lies.

56

They call him Robertito, as if to underscore the difference between his size and his mind. He's tall and large, with the strength of a horse. His strides are long, somewhat open, which makes his torso sway from side to side. His flaccid arms follow that rhythm, as if from that swaying all his vitality emerges. His mouth is half-open. The sounds that he makes are expressive, though he never pronounces anything that even resembles a word.

He arrives at dawn and stands there watching me, emitting sounds. I give him bread to silence him. He eats standing up. He devours. Even then he babbles, but much less. He makes a funny face that resembles a smile. I gesture to him to move away, because the clients are going to come. He broadens his grin and nods. He walks backward and remains against the wall, near the corner, until don Victor indicates to him with a brief sign that they're going to leave. He doesn't leave without flapping a hand as a sign of farewell. Clumsily each time. And they go out so many times a day.

One Sunday don Victor lets me go to the river. He warns me that in winter the water's not very high, that the river banks are rocky and foliage is yellow.

We travel in the truck with Robertito along a dirt path that crosses pastures and cultivated fields. I ask him if these are his lands. He doesn't answer me. With his hand, he indicates the direction in which I should walk and obliges me to get out of the truck. He honks the horn three times. When I hear it again, I have to run to reach it. If not, I have to figure out a way to return on foot before nightfall. He doesn't know that, in that moment, the path to the river is etched on my memory like a tattoo.

I pass through the branches of willows. The song of the water is metallic, contained in a profound crease of its own creation. Verdant serpent that doesn't look at the sky nor at the willows that tinge the ever-changing surface.

One morning when the previous night's rain continues and the clouds have transformed into an iron curtain, a gentleman approaches the counter. Both his hair and his clothing are youthful, but that doesn't hide the fact that he's middle-aged. He unfolds before me a paper he calls "official." That small piece of paper authorizes him to inspect the wine cellar and seize whatever he finds. I tell him that I don't have the keys, that there's nothing there, that I don't know how to distinguish official stamps, that nobody authorized me to allow him to go in there, that he should come later, that I don't know anything.

Regardless, he signals two guys who are waiting outside and they go into the hallway. They remove the hinges from each door. I want to ask for help but I can't leave the store abandoned with the men inside. I'm not about to scream in the street. They might take me to jail or don Victor might get angry because I made a scene in front of his store. So I just stand there watching them enter his dusty wine cellars and scratch the already disintegrating walls. They also go into my room. They inspect everything and open the armoire. I'm embarrassed by the solitude of the dress and that hanging apron. They don't close the door and they turn around in the hallway uttering angry words. I ask them to straighten out the disorder that they've created. They answer me with a number of threats toward don Victor and then leave.

My face is weepy when don Victor and Robertito return. I tell them what happened. I already forgot the words they used and my flimsy voice doesn't succeed in impressing the tone or the force with which the men spoke. I ask forgiveness for the broken doors. Robertito caresses my cheek with surprising gentleness. Don Victor explains to him how to fix the doors. He walks to the counter, whistling. Some clients arrive and he begins to tell them, entertained, what's happened. They start laughing. They glance at me sideways. I only understand that it's going to be a long day, with so many people coming and going and making fun of me.

I don't have a nightgown, so I sleep in an old dress of Amelia's. I'm in the dark. He enters. He pulls down the covers and begins to fondle me. I don't move. His hand gets lost among my thighs. A finger forages around that soft, absorbent tunnel.

"How do you do it, make it close up each time?" he pants in my ear.

He smells of bitter wine. His warmth moistens my ear and fills it with murky words. He asks me to whisper sweet nothings, so that they shower him with my cascading voice and spill over into his ears, overflowing with the filthy phrases he's taught me.

I cross my legs. I want to say that I don't like San Juan, that I'm forgetting how the leaves are braided by the wind, that the song and the earthly aromas have been removed from these odorless torrents of water, that the strained air of these rooms doesn't caress or accompany my footsteps as once did that wind heavy with dust. I want to scream at him that I don't understand people; that I'm afraid of words and silence; that all the spaces are oc-

58

cupied; and that moving or still, I'm always in a hole that doesn't belong to me; that I tremble at the touch of each day that passes.

But instead, I ask him to take me to the river on Sunday. And when he promises, I open my legs and my mouth and repeat those words I've learned.

The guy who was insulting accused don Victor of being involved in the black market. The idea keeps circling around in my head. Black market. I imagine a fair where dark cloths are spread out. On top of them, bones, spiders, evil powders, devil's hair. To the rear, canvas tents where spells are cast, and one finds burning pots, bubbling liquids, dolls with a rigid and terrorizing expression, prayers and songs, rites and sacrifices. Each night I tremble. Between dreams and drowsiness, don Victor's gaze appears before me, bloodstained and brilliant; his laughter becomes sinister and the recollection of his body inclined over the back of a client reveals conspiracies and contempt more dreadful than I can conceive.

Day arrives and fear dissolves under the icy water. But the trembling in my heart remains as a result of the disquieting night.

One afternoon I ask him why they said that about him. I said it just like that, carelessly, as if I'd not spent hours rehearsing it. His gaze doesn't cloud over nor does he bend over cursing me. Unscrupulously he explains to me what businessmen call "going on the defense" in terms of their stores. Merchandise arrives late and in unsatisfactory condition from the factories and one must sell it at a reducd price. And the second order, when it dignifies itself to appear, has a much higher value. How is one going to pay in cash with what one has saved if it isn't a sufficient amount? It's a whirlwind into which one should never fall. It's for that very reason that many businessmen ration their products and sell them at a higher price. Their sole purpose is to save their businesses. It's not sabotage, as many contend. They're producing less than what's needed. The sellers aren't guilty nor are they willing to allow themselves to be ruined so others can fill their pockets. Something similar happens with the land's harvest. The farmers are expected to deliver these at a shamefully low price but then they don't have anything with which to sow the fields or feed their livestock. He gets worked up and strikes the table, but ends up laughing upon remembering the many times an official has inspected his wine cellars, reviewed his receipts and every other little thing his tiny brain is capable of inventing. As if the merchandise wasn't fought over and the pantries emptied before he wanted them to be. As if he's so naïve he'd stock his store with goods that are supposedly unattainable. Official papers speak in the voice that suits them. In any case, he's doing the country a favor if the officials realize their error and return to their slums.

That's why he comes and goes to his businesses with Robertito—a strong idiot of a man who can't betray him. Even though I don't understand anything, upon seeing him fling himself on my bed bursting with pride, my impression is that I no longer distinguish the contours of things. Dazed, I fall by his side.

Don Victor goes to mass at noon on Sunday. The day I arrived, he told me to go to mass on Saturday at dusk. At that hour the old women who never miss a mass are in attendance. They cover their heads and their lips move swiftly and endlessly. I enter the church early. The line for the confessional is tapering off. I go to the end of the line, distancing myself and keeping somewhat toward the side. People kneel. I hear murmuring. I keep giving up my turn until the little intricate lattice-work window is closed. The priest emerges and looks all around. He notices me, as if to ask me or invite me to purge my soul. I shake my head and make a face that feigns a smile of gratitude. The priest no longer looks at me. As I sit seated on the wooden pew, thoughts that I'd like to smooth out and dissect, fasten to a loom and weave together until they appear in the fabric as a picture I've never seen, become all tangled and confused.

Don Victor doesn't come with me to the river. He drops me off and leaves. It's better that way. I don't need anyone to accompany me. He spends the days, and perhaps the nights, working far away. Hurriedly. Because the party's almost over, he says. And then he'll need the money in his hands to purchase land the peasants won't be capable of exploiting.

I sit down on the damp and cool rocks. Meters below, the water lashes the riverbanks. Sometimes I braid branches of willow. Other times, I throw small stones into the river and watch them sink. I also walk against the wind until I'm exhausted. Then I sit down again and eat the bread, nuts, or whatever I've brought with me.

I no longer play with numbers. Nor do I knit. I spend hours behind an empty counter, longing to go toss little stones in a river.

60

Nights are long. I try to separate the sounds coming from the street. At times I distinguish those of cars and trucks. The rest are confused murmurs. Except the church bells.

It's late. A Saturday evening. The sky is darkening. I'm lowering the metal curtain. When the lock has been placed, the day will have ended. Don Victor's at a political meeting. The street's empty. I hear music in the distance. A star flickers among the streetlights. I close the lock. Standing on the outside of the store, the keys fall into my pocket. I loosen my hair from its ribbons and it tumbles down my back. It sways to the rhythm of my small steps. Slowly I arrive at the plaza. The lights are on. A song emerges from beneath the gazebo. It's an ear-piercing record. Then it changes. They alternate incessantly. Desperation, encounters, deceits . . . each sentiment disquiets me. My face is uncontrollable, making awkward expressions. Among the bushes I shiver in the cold. People stroll along the sidewalk, circling the plaza. At times, they linger. Converse. Then they keep walking. Their faces are identical. They smile. They spin around, looking behind them. They make comments. The music never stops. Nor do those gloomy gestures.

One morning I can't raise the metal curtain. When it's halfway up, disorder erupts, a combination of cutting voices and the balmy dawn of spring. Something unfamiliar to me snaps and crackles. I'm in darkness for two days, two nights, I don't know. The silence surrounding me is so solid that I walk barefoot between my room and the store, shrouded in shadows.

Another dawn comes and he raises the curtain. The street begins to babble. The sun is up high, indifferent to the weariness in which the pavements are wrapped. His entrance is noisy. He tells me how the experiment ended. The failure of stupidity. In the capital and the provinces, in a matter of hours, they swept away the opportunists. Suddenly, unexpectedly the streets were cleared and now martial law will extend to the farthest corners of the land.

I don't understand what's happened. The days are brief. People come near the store to look at the shelves, which begin to be filled. They continue sitting at the tables, but they no longer shout and boast. Small groups murmur after first glancing all around them. Some have stopped coming. Things are said about them and their families. There's a rift between others. Not really a dividing line, rather like a tear in a piece of silk fabric which frays into unpredictable curves.

I keep serving and waiting on the clients. Silently. We close early. It's not permitted to go out at night, so the sun sets when the door latches fall.

Don Victor's truck is now kept in the patio in the interior of the store. Some evenings I hear distant voices and the engine starting. Hours later, I'm awakened by his return. There are no longer other voices. It seems like only the driver returns.

I remain there with my eyes wide open. I'm waiting for something. Nothing happens. Dawn slips away.

Mrs. Gabriela is one of many of the women who shop at the store. She lives a few blocks away. She produces jams and sweets with the fruits from the farm her husband cultivates.

It's been very hot the afternoon she enters. Her cheeks are sunken and her eyes are shining. She approaches don Victor. She speaks to him in a hushed, pleading tone. Nonetheless, I manage to hear fragments. She asks him to intercede with his friends so they can give her news about her husband. She knows nothing about him since the day they took him to answer some questions. Now they're denying that he's detained. She's imploring him by virtue of the cordial relationship that they've maintained throughout these years and of the desperation that compels her to knock on every door.

Don Victor listens to her without interrupting. He nods in understanding. He urges her to continue talking. When finally the sobs have silenced her voice, he tells her that he can't do anything. She insists.

"But if you ask them, I'll know where he is. Just that."

Don Victor tells her that she should have faith. If the man is innocent, they won't keep him long. He calmly tells her to go home, that everything's in order.

"And who can tell me what's innocence for them? Perhaps they'll find me guilty for having supported the deceased president. We liked his way of thinking and Mario's not of the kind to remain silent. And if there's no harm in thinking while continuing to work, doing no harm to others . . . "

Tersely, don Victor repeats that she should go and await the news that will be arriving. The woman stands up and discovers in his eyes an icy gaze, his pupils contracted and cutting. Doña Gabriela pulls herself together and with a step forward attempts to appear steadfast, although her entire body reflects the dejection of that senseless humiliation.

The river has risen. It hums along and moves suggestively, like the young girls who arrive on its banks and bend to gather fresh water, the water that's the pretext to walk among the sown fields with their dresses swaying in the wind.

A deep pool has formed in one of the bends of the river. I sit down on one of the rocks and let my feet become chilled, submerged in the water. Children come to bathe. They splash me with their games. I, too, splash with my hands. They aren't looking at me, so I lift up my skirt and get soaked up to my waist. Squatting, the little stones from the depths of the river etching themselves on my skin, I doze off to sleep, not feeling the contrast between the icy water and the sun burning my back.

We've already closed, but they remain seated at the table on which bottles continue to pile up. Their uniform jackets are carefully placed on the backs of the chairs. Their shirts, however, are open at the neck and their shirttails untucked. Their pant legs are wrinkled.

The uproar doesn't stop. They're drunk. So is don Victor, though not as much as the others. They say stupidities, curse, scream and bellow, and end up laughing. Two of them smoke. I empty the ashtrays when I approach the table with another bottle. One of those who smokes seems to be the boss of the others or something like that. He's slender. His hair is short and very black. A beaked nose. Clean shaven. Inflamed eyes. He grabs me by the waist and asks don Victor why he's hired this skinny girl instead of a real woman, what with all the female prisoners available. He speaks with gestures. He draws a figure in the air. He repeats it several times increasing its glamour. He stands up and, staggering, begins to run his firm hands all over me, fingers pointed like the claws of a condor. He screams about what I'm missing here and there. He tells me that to be a real woman, I need to know the pleasure men give.

"I could do that favor for you," he pants.

The others laugh. They celebrate his generosity. Voices are confused. He presses against my buttocks. His hand gets lost under my dress. He mutters that I should invite him to my room, that I'm going to have the privilege of being initiated with an expert, that my legs are going to open up all by themselves.

"You're going to beg me for more." His voice sounds high-pitched: "Give me more of your delicious milk, do it harder, more."

They applaud him. They laugh imitating the movements of a women being possessed. The thin guy remains standing with his hand between my legs. The words incite him.

"I'll be back soon," he tells them while he walks and pushes me toward the hallway. "Don't drink it all. I'm going to be thirsty after I fulfill this duty."

"To the health of the hero!" someone shouts.

They clink their glasses. Before I become lost in the darkness, I spin my head around. I search for the glance of don Victor. There it is.

It's no different than the others'.

Summer drives me crazy. Before he takes possession of the houses or the sheaves turn golden, don Victor departs. He announces it to me the day before he leaves. Perhaps he goes to Pedregal. Maybe. I know he'll go. He doesn't offer to take anything special from me to my family. He denies me the possibility of even telling them that I'm not sending anything because I didn't have time to prepare anything for them.

He informs me he'll return after Christmas. He takes out his wallet and offers me money to buy myself a present. "I only want a window," I tell him after I have the money in my pocket. He laughs. Lately he either laughs or becomes infuriated. You can never tell. This time laughter emerges. He summons Robertito and speaks to him. They come to my room. Robertito pounds the wall that don Victor indicates to him. He uses a short hammer and an iron.

"Sledge hammer and chisel," indicates don Victor.

He stands with his hands in his pockets while Robertito opens the hole. In no time light floods the room. Through the uneven edges of the opening, I can see the interior patio of the store. And beyond that, I hear the sounds from the street.

"Later we'll put in a frame and glass. For now, you don't need them."

I nod in agreement several times. I can hardly control the smile provoked by the wind as it caresses the back of my neck.

That night, don Victor takes a chair from the corner and places it next to the window. He sits with his pants open. He lowers them to his ankles. I sit on top of him. We are both looking in the same direction. The warmth of his words wanders along my shoulders and glides down my back, which ascends and descends, rhythmically, like the gait of young girls. He tells me to imagine that he's not there, that it's another who's taking me from behind; he makes me tell him what he's like, what he asks me, how our bodies merge, how profoundly he fits into the most remote spaces. He pants while I talk. Through the thickness of my hair, I give my voice all the intonations possible, I make it dance along the walls so the air becomes emotionally charged and compresses upon him until it bursts and gushes forth, dissolves in the last moan and, finally falling silent, gives way to the tune of the streets.

Every afternoon I collect the money from the cash register. I place it in a box, along with any tickets and receipts that may have come in that day. Robertito carries it to the accountant. He brings the box back to me empty or with a piece of paper on which he's written a question or a request for a certain document or an explanation. The accountant's handwriting is spiky and convoluted. I later learn that it's his assistant who writes the notes. Perhaps I should add his female assistant. It's all the same. His silent missives and Robertito's noisy grimaces are my contact with what's beyond the metal curtain.

The people who come to buy don't converse with me. Nor do I know how to initiate a dialogue. Nevertheless, the people in front of the counter converse effortlessly among themselves. At times they murmur. I can't hear what they're saying. Sometimes the entrance of someone silences the others. I'd like to know what happens upon passing through the door into the store. I don't know how to arrive. Nor how to leave.

The hours are protracted, the days confused. I'm in San Juan. Spinning among the walls. Going from one lifeless point to another.

I've exchanged my apron for a dress. I wear my hair down. I still haven't decided if I'll go with a bun or braids to Christmas mass.

He pokes his head through my new window. He looks different. He no longer has a mustache. He's grown thin. In spite of the darkness, I see that his eyes still sparkle. He asks me about don Victor. I tell him what I know. I invite him to come in. I offer him water. And almonds. He crushes the shells with his teeth. Then he peels them with his fingers. He asks me to eat with him. I refuse with a shake of my head. The almonds crunch in his mouth. He explains to me that don Victor is his father, that I shouldn't say anything to anyone about his being here, that we'll open one of the wine cellars so he can get settled but meanwhile I need not worry, that he's going to tell his father that I didn't have any alternative other than receiving him,

65

in spite of being of stranger. He speaks and walks toward the darkened hallway. I follow behind. Manuel doesn't recognize me.

The days between parties gallop along hallways that are no longer dark. Two blocks of wood support light bulbs that he never extinguishes. His door opens countless times. When he's alone, he leaves it ajar. They seek him from the interior patio. Then he knocks on the wall in the manner we've established and I look out my window. The visitor tells me the phrase I need to hear and I allow him to enter, crossing through my room. They buy me cookies and bread. Sometimes cold cuts or cheese. I heat water for them on my brazier and then I wash the cups. He thanks me. I try to go and fetch the dirty dishes when he's alone so I can listen to him. He discusses difficulties and satisfactions. Briefly. I think he knows that I don't understand what's happening. That's why he's so open with me.

I fall asleep at any hour. The clarity of the moon embraces me and the murmur of their voices leads me to lose myself in a snug, still sleepiness.

I ask him if he wants anything special for New Year's Eve. He responds that the year that's passing was bleak, that it opened a grave into which many were still about to fall.

I create a little doll out of straw. I dress it with the pockets of an old dress. I snip a lock of my hair for her. A piece of paper is all I need to make a hat. With scraps of wool, I weave a scarf and give it to him and wait to see if he asks me to put it on him.

"Burn the old year . . ." he smiles. I no longer remembered that custom of the countryside. A totem taller than the tallest of men, flames caressing it and in the silence of the night, only the crackling of the fire is heard. The totem's eyes reflect the flames and are abruptly extinguished as the ashes turn black. Only then does the party begin, when the wind has carried away the smoke of so many sorrows.

We place the doll in a basin on the small heater. Before midnight, he lights it. It's consumed in a matter of seconds. It falls. The ashes collapse. The smoke doesn't rise. Enclosed in his room, he whirs around the embers, as if he feared distancing himself from that semi-vacant basin.

His face becomes gloomy. He asks me to leave. He says, "I'm waiting for someone."

I go to my room. The bells toll and I'm clinging tenaciously to the frame of the door, watching him walk down the hallway toward the store. I

66

hear the echo of the chimes at the same time the metal curtain's raised. I close my door so I'm not seen. The steps that return are soft, almost soundless, taken close to one another. Hushed murmurs. Attentive and gleeful. Within seconds, the hallway fills with an emotion with which I'm unfamiliar, but that should have the force of fusion, of the postponed encounter, of sentiments of whatever origin becoming blended, rejected, magnetized, creating in each touch the irreplaceable fragment of something that never stops shaping itself.

He bumps against the door while he closes it. The key jingles when he turns it in the lock.

How the armoire groans!

The girl is named Erika. The name doesn't suit her, so he calls her Paloma. He says to her, "My Paloma has finally arrived." She comes at dawn or at the hour of the afternoon nap. She brings papers, newspaper clippings, leaflets. She departs with others. She returns when the sun's set. They speak hurriedly. I'm not sure what they say. Words flow between them. There's almost always someone else. Some come, others go. They also speak with urgency. Men and women in the same tone.

The week is flying by. My days crawl between the counter and the shelves. Now it's the young girl who brings him pots and small packages. I have given them my brazier which, at any rate, isn't even mine. I've not accepted an invitation to eat with them. I sit with Robertito on the patio. He devours bread with something and I try to swallow pieces of fruit. We look at the truck. The sun heats the soles of my shoes. Upon standing, a dry heat seems to deter my steps. I walk slowly toward the counter. I no longer have the radio. Manuel asked me for it so often that I told him to keep it, that I'll take it back when I need it. Not once have I asked him for it. I wouldn't know how to say I *need* it. Those words sound pitiful in my mouth. When he says *need* he's saying *important*.

He speaks with a gentle and profound voice. Each syllable is drawn from the depths of his being, a profound sense of sadness that springs from his soul bleeding and warm and doesn't stop beating between my outstretched hands.

The words ooze out of Manuel like they did with the ink that day he's already forgotten. I still keep the stain. It's no longer black and has become trimmed with an ochre color that will eventually devour it. It's difficult for me to grasp what he's saying. To grasp it in time to write it down on paper.

"Everyone, in the eyes of everyone, is responsible for everything."

"Justice exists and one doesn't pass from it to its opposite; only through injustice, with all of its narrowness and difficulties, can we approach that ideal."

"Rifles are noisy but are filled with silence."

"It doesn't matter that the song be stifled by walls. Man sings in search of solace, to find encouragement when he's feeling defeated, to accompany the one who's marching forward and the one who, perhaps, we'll never see again. The song of men will continue in the wind as long as we exist."

"It's all so absurd; we can't permit pain to remain distant and our eyes to be diverted from that which hurts them."

"It doesn't matter if the farewell is somber or not what we desired; what matters is that we're bidding farewell to a life that's been happy to achieve the realization of how we wish to live and die."

"Try to find the tenderness of remembrance and discard the cruelty of memory."

He laughs when I tell him that I write down his words and wish that he'd say them more slowly so that not a single one slips away from me. He tells me that they're all in books. They begin there and develop in the interior of each man and meld with others. He lends me some books. A stack of silent paper. I don't open them.

The curtain is already drawn when don Victor. arrives. His presence fills the spaces much more than the lights that illuminate the hallway. He retreats with Manuel to the empty wine cellar.

Useless door.

He rants in such a way that each word makes the walls shake. He tells him that his battles are effortless when one has a father upon whom he can lean. After the first difficulty, call Papa, yet criticize his way of living. Despise his beliefs but not his money or his home.

Manuel answers without getting agitated. He promises to go away soon. He explains that right now the situation is dangerous for many people. He speaks of detainees, of the dead, of the need to not abandon oneself to nostalgia or fear. That he didn't want to be at his beck and call, that he prefers to arrive at a compromise with himself and help others before he becomes entangled in pointless pride. And, as a son and a man, he doesn't reject him. His thoughts are divergent; it's just that. And nothing more than that.

Don Victor speaks about his prestige, of the savings that he's ammassed, the money Manuel finds so disgusting, yet he depends upon all that Papa has achieved. It will be his inheritance, that filthy cash that supports him and permits him to play the hero while others work and produce. They argue. Nevertheless Manuel can stay if he complies with his father's demands. No clandestine activities nor questionable friendships. Manuel accepts with excessive haste. That means he's not going to obey his father.

Robertito levels the opening in the wall in my room and hammers strips of wood into the edges. Leaning against that frame is a window that opens toward the interior. The glass is thick, opaque, and has a rough texture. With the window closed I can't see the patio, only the silhouette of light.

He spends two afternoons gluing and pasting wallpaper. White. With tiny bouquets of pink and cerulean flowers. The smell of the glue lingers after Robertito leaves.

My room is now diaphanous. Don Victor enters. He eventually falls asleep. His figure fractures the bright whiteness of the room. He flails with abandonment amid the floral images on the wall. His jowls settle upon his chest. An enormous stain of obscurity. His snoring shatters the silence. There I am, stretched out beside him like always. The walls resemble the horizon above his silhouette. It doesn't matter when he takes me because I'm entangled in my hair and his grunts flood my ears, but in the moments of rest, my body's exhausted.

Manuel is compiling papers in his room. He writes letters and then copies them. Blue ink upon greenish paper. He receives mail in a box at the post office. He reads the letters and discards them, or keeps them, or copies them. There's nothing on the envelopes that would allow anyone to know their origination. Envelopes of many sizes and thicknesses. Previously his friends or the girl brought them to him and then carried them away. Now some of them are being followed. He asks me to go to the post office. As soon as don Victor leaves, I lower the curtain and run across the back patio. I race down the sidewalk to the post office and get in line. Then I dash back home, clutching the documents.

Robertito also receives assignments. I ask Manuel if he can be trusted. If not, he's making a major mistake and runs the risk of being de-

69

nounced. He tells me that he's known Robertito since they were children and that they used to fish together on the banks of the river. That back then, Robertito was smarter than anyone in school or in the fields. One afternoon he climbed up to the bell tower of the church and fell from the belfry. Nobody saw the accident. Some elderly women found him on their way to mass. They thought they wouldn't be able to save him. The blow to his head affected his speech and motor coordination, but his mind was still alert and his sensitivity permeable to the emotions he's denied.

"People forget and now they treat him as if he were an idiot."

He explains that his father hired him and pays him a miserable salary, paying him when he remembers, not respecting the number of hours that he has to work and disregarding the law. He uses him because it's convenient to have him, but he never tires of reiterating that if it weren't for him, Robertito would be indigent, begging in the plaza.

"His interior being is intact," he concludes.

Later I listen to Manuel speak to him. The same voice, calling him Roberto. A respectful tone. His words. And I, behind the counter, pretend to be busy filing sales slips so I can't raise my eyes and see the transparent gaze of his eyes reflecting my shameful image.

Don Victor brings me some dresses. They're colorful and the fabric is soft and sheer, although somewhat cold to the touch. They slide down my body, clinging to my form and distancing me from him.

Summer is fading the night he invites me to go out with him. He tells me he has much to celebrate. The sale of his harvested crops and something else. I climb into the truck. He drives erratically. We head toward the outskirts of San Juan. He stops in front of a house with balconies. We get out of the truck. He enters and I follow behind. It takes me a while to become accustomed to the darkness. the parlors are filled with men and women in an attitude of total abandonment. They're smoking and drinking, their inebriated bodies incongruous to their laughter. I'm not sure where the music is coming from. A woman greets him. She barely acknowledges me. We ascend to the rooms above.

"Totally private," the women assures him.

It's a beautiful bedroom. Don Victor stands on the threshold. He's paying her. He also murmurs something. When we're alone, he doesn't touch me. He sits in an armchair and lights a cigarette. The door opens and a young women with fair hair enters. She smiles at him and scrutinizes me. She approaches. She undoes the buttons of my dress until it falls to the floor. She caresses me while she removes the rest of my clothing. I'm naked when she loosens my hair. Her hands get lost in my tresses and touch skin that's aroused by her touch. She unties the sash of her dress. Her body is revealed within a matter of seconds. Even though she's thin, her curves and ridges undulate aggressively. She forces herself on me and presses her breasts against me. She proceeds to force open my legs. We're still standing, her hands having explored all my intimate parts. Don Victor is collapsed in the armchair. He's opened his shirt and his hand is excited between his legs. He watches us. His eyes are expressionless. The young woman coaxes me to extend myself on the bed. The time elapsed between her caresses and the enveloping perfume seems like forever. She guides my hands along a descending path. The moistness between us becomes one, and I begin to lose myself in the tangle of her hair with mine. Over there, he comes, grazing me with his gaze.

The sky's gray. There was a threat of rain a couple of days ago, but nothing happened. I'm helping a lady when Esther enters. She makes a gesture and waits.

Robertito looks at her and attempts to smile at her from among the jars he's unpacking. She waves her hand in a sign of greeting. She moves about the store examining every corner. The curiosity in her eyes is routine, disinterested, just like the smile that's etched joylessly on her face. Her skin has turned opaque, even though it's still smooth. Her beauty has changed but she still attracts attention, gazes at her striking figure.

We're finally alone. She tells me that things have become more difficult for her. I laugh. For Esther it's not about things, circumstances. The path. Impatience drives her. She pretends to be angry at my laughter. She then hugs me tightly.

"You can't even imagine all we've been through." She then relates the way in which they were stripped, the humiliation and harassment to which some of the women were subjected, the punishment meted out to the men.

"And, above all, the fear. You have no idea what fear is."

Her eyes are teary. I want to tell her that, indeed, I do know what fear is. And worst of all is that there's no reason to be subjected to acts so often that you begin to agonize over fear itself. But I don't say a single word. I just keep looking at her and stroking her hair awkwardly.

She tells me that from the town where she was with Pablo, she returned to Pedregal. That she reconciled with our father and that she's now living there with Pablo.

"We're getting married," she says with a smile.

I ask her why. She shrugs her shoulders. She supposes that her time has come. I insist. She used to say it wasn't necessary to sign a document to assure love, that feelings are like birds, they wither and fade when confined to a cage. She now finds that within established norms, there are important inherent values. The opinion that others have of her matter. She wants to be accepted in the tiny recesses of that remote landscape.

"I came to buy my trousseau and other items needed in the countryside. And to find out about you. Our father wants to know. And I want you to attend the wedding. It will take place in April."

I merely want to know, I need to know, what became of the chants that hovered over the hills, of the young men that roamed the land and didn't covet it, of the voices that tugged at sunken chests and straightened backs bent and broken by physical labor, of the gazes that saw the turn in the path ahead of their light steps, of the nights when the moon wasn't needed to walk beneath the stars.

She explains to me that those were ideals that were unattainable, that one has to adapt to change and reversals. She asks me to stop talking and accompany her to the stores, to ask don Victor if he'll allow her to stay with me a couple of nights, to cheer up and accompany her and fill the streets with our laughter.

The sky's painted black and blue, as if it were a crow flying over the treetops. The stores have been closing one by one. We stop to rest in the plaza. We place the bags at our feet. I ask her where she obtained so much money. She replies something like an inheritance from the past; each time the words are more elusive, like those of Manuel. They seep through every layer of my skin and flit about like a flock of sparrows. I try to explain that to her. She interrupts me with a laugh.

"You've fallen in love with him!"

"No, it's not that."

I wouldn't want to cling to his body or feel warmth at the gentle touch of his hands. I don't dream about his breath in my ears, weaving whispers and sighs. Nor would I want to tremble beneath the weight of his passion overwhelming me, his head buried in my hair, to then have him turn away and fall asleep in silence. I just aspire to wash his dishes and to catch the words that spill forth.

But she doesn't understand me. Or I simply don't know how to express myself adequately. It's difficult to translate colors into words.

Manuel and Esther speak for a moment. He remembers Pablo vaguely. Nonetheless he's interested in knowing what's become of him and of so many others. My sister responds in a brief, harsh way.

She opens the packages in my room, placing the items she's purchased on top of my bed. She lists the items still missing. I want to know what she thinks of Manuel. To see him with distant eyes. She tells me that she's no longer interested in his type, that she's moved on past that stage and isn't willing to give her life for lost causes. Besides, it may now be dangerous to interact with those who haven't accepted defeat.

"Ultimately, one has to learn to look out for oneself."

I'm overcome with a swell of emotions. They slowly recede and fade away. The flood of emotions bears no resemblance to what I feel inside. Esther looks at me with worry.

"All this is going to cause you great harm, little one. A woman should never pursue a gentleman of another socioeconomic class. Especially when the differences are so pronounced."

I help her pack the items she can't stop caressing. We speak about the metals that don't rust, the fabrics that almost never wrinkle, the knitted pieces made from a wool that's not wool. I barely speak. I fall asleep promising her that I'm going to attend the wedding, even though I have no idea how I'll be able go.

Robertito and I are on the patio. He takes down the crates of tomatoes while I make a note of the quantity. It's the time when everyone takes a siesta, so there's no noise coming from the street.

Suddenly don Victor arrives. His truck almost rolls over the tomatoes. He descends from the truck furious and storms into the store without looking at us. The screams that come from Manuel's room shake the stillness of the walls. He tells him that they caught a subversive and that among his papers were some that tied him to Manuel. What was he doing casting doubt on his honor in the eyes of others, tarnishing the good name for which he's worked so hard? He breaks things, rummages through papers. He doesn't stop screaming. He prohibits anyone from visiting Manuel, although they've diminished in numbers to the point that they almost no longer exist. He enters the patio carrying reams of crumpled papers. He lights a fire. He tells me I'm stupid, that he's going to throw me out into the street if I continue to run errands for his son. I respond that I don't know anything, that I rarely speak with him, that I have no knowledge of the correspondence, that I never leave the store. He also reproaches Robertito, who doesn't respond, merely looks at him disconcertedly. Don Victor insists that he's surrounded by idiots and traitors. His face turns red with rage. His bulging cheeks sag every time he leans down to relight the fire. His pupils are tinged with bluish flame. Between the smoke and the insults, what clearly rises is his fear.

The nights are getting colder. I have my mother's blanket and shawl. I tell don Victor I'm going to need more layers in the coming winter.

"I don't like women wrapped up in rags."

He instructs me to take off my clothes. I'm shivering in the center of the room. He forces me onto the bed, face down. I'm still trembling. Brief shudders shake my entire body when he begins to strike with a leather belt.

"Scream when you're no longer cold!"

I don't raise my voice. I murmur that it's enough, that I'm hot. He places his hand between my legs. His fingers thrust inside me. He asks me if the heat is extinguished up there. I tell him that no, that my body is burning. I cover my face, but he doesn't touch me. He goes to the bathroom and brings back a bottle of cologne. The top of the bottle comes off easily. With one hand he holds the bottle of cologne and with the fingers of his other hand he opens my vagina, which is now a receptacle, and he pours the cold cologne inside me. In an instant it becomes warm and then begins to burn. The scent is a heavy breath among the walls. Organs that I'd never felt become inflamed and palpitate. A veritable brazier in my abdomen. I want to stop screaming but I can't, so he stifles me with a pillow.

I awaken several times that night. My own moans keep me from sleeping. It no longer hurts as much but anguish is spreading throughout my chest.

Manuel tells me that he's going to leave soon. Here he's losing himself and feels fenced in. He's not going to wait for events to move him. He'll set out on a journey and try to change things at the source of the problem.

I ask him when he's leaving.

"Not yet, but soon."

I think about myself, how I've never gone to a place where I wanted to be. But I haven't desired anything either. Perhaps there's been a vague notion about the necessity of fleeing without knowing from what. Running blindly from one darkness to another.

The bank of the river. I stray from the usual path. Beyond the weeping willows, I can see houses distinct from one another. Some children are searching for toads among the stones. I ask them if they know which house belongs to don Victor. They don't know. I continue along the path and ask the same question to a couple of peasants. They tell me that I'm close and indicate the road. I find a woman harvesting herbs from a garden. I don't interrupt her work to ask her to show me where his land begins and to indicate the extent of it. Immense green pastures. The house is one story and extends toward an expansive garden that's well maintained and inviting. Through the window, I see the silhouette of someone moving back and forth in a room. I ask the woman if she knows who's moving about in that house. She turns her head to the north and continues to bend over toward the earth.

"It must be his wife."

I'm not able to distinguish her appearance. I don't care. She's surely elegant, I tell myself. Just by the beauty of her home. And they surely have been together for years. That garden was not planted recently.

I return by way of the road the river designed. It's getting dark as I cross the plaza of San Juan.

I'm alone as I cross the plaza. I step on the leaves that fall silently. The rustle made by my feet treading over them sends a warmth up through my back. But there it stays and begins to freeze. A cold that's biting and profoundly discomforting. I go up the steps to the church. I stand before the flapping doors. People avoid me and keep the doors moving. Nobody leaves. It's as if they were being inhaled by a gust of wind into the mouth of a tunnel. I've crossed this threshold so many times without thinking. Even now I'm not thinking. Simply immobilized. I retreat. I bump into a woman. I ask her forgiveness in an unintelligible manner. I turn around and begin to run. The wind is calm, but its moans shake my entire body. Panting, I fall onto my bed and into a profound sleep.

The sound of a motor awakens me. I'm drifting back into sleep when I hear footsteps. The clicking of heels in the hallway stops in front of Manuel's room. I hear the voices of men, but not their words. In a matter of minutes they depart. The car's engine is started, its roar is lost in the night.

I walk toward the door of his room. It's open. There's no one inside. The bed is unmade. His watch is there on the chair, next to the radio. It's three in the morning.

I can't sleep that night.

I tell don Victor his son is gone. He replies that it doesn't surprise him, as that's how he is. I persist. I tell him I heard footsteps, that some men took him away.

"What men would those be? Surely his own friends!" and he tells me that since they're involved in all kinds of schemes, they move about at the strangest hours.

But the uneasiness I feel today is similar to that of yesterday. Misfortunes are crowned by a bitter aura that lasts longer than the misfortune itself. Strands of anguish begin knitting a cloth that, at dusk, is so dense that air can barely reach my body.

The hallway is the tangled trace of a forest and it leads to the marsh of my room.

On Sunday I approach the home of Mrs. Gabriela. I tell her about Manuel. We speak on the threshold of her house. She doesn't invite me inside. Briefly she tells me that they're not going to lay a hand on don Victor's son. Her tone is bitter and blunt. I want to ask about her husband. I don't as I know the response. She asks me to leave. I spend the afternoon wandering through the streets, hoping to find a familiar face that can commiserate with me and my doubts.

The days strip away time. Endless nights are consumed. Stretched out on my bed, I look around. The flowers on the wallpaper form branches. Four different branches are repeated in a pattern. I find figures in them. They're not always immediately discernible. My hands grasp the blanket as I lie in wait. My eyes seek them out. And there's the figure. My hands relax.

Upon turning the corner, I see her silhouette. I might say that I intuit it from afar. I run to her. I'm not sure if I should call her Erika or Paloma, so I say nothing. I touch her shoulder. We look at each other. With-

76

out even greeting her, I ask her about him. Her response is cold.

"As if you didn't know," she says.

Weeks of anguish overcome me. I clutch her arm and beg for an answer. I know my words are unintelligible among the sobs. She's disconcerted. Just for a moment. Then she looks at me with the disgust reserved for someone who isn't worth anything, someone who's willing to stoop to the lowest level to remain afloat, like rubbish in the water.

She mumbles insults and says, "So many have fallen after being denounced by cowards. Even the silent ones are guilty."

She tries to push me away so I can no longer touch her. I clutch her with even greater strength. My voice is barely audible, and I plead with her to forgive me. She manages to wrest herself from my grasp. She's repulsed by the touch of someone who's remained close to a father so vile, a father capable of doing that.

She moves away. She says something about all that will no longer be. My soft and urgent tone has changed her. She speaks hurriedly, wanting to tear herself away. Her thoughts become tangled and weak and surface as murky and gravelly words. She walks away, projecting a protracted shadow that casts a black tinge over the sidewalk.

I'm still standing. My arms hang by my side. People walk past in one direction or another. The wind hasn't changed. The clouds don't form new figures in the sky. I'm faced with a row of closed doors.

There are thoughts that come to be more significant than the body that contains them. I have barely any ideas my head, and I don't know how to put the static ideas in my gut into movement.

I have to leave. I already know that. Perhaps to Pedregal. Surely Esther has already married. Or to another town. It would be easy if I didn't have to drag myself to other places.

I ask Robertito if we can go to the river on Sunday. I don't understand his response, but before the bells ring for the first mass, he knocks on the window of my room.

He's wearing clothing that I 've never seen before. We make the journey in silence. The top of my head doesn't even reach his shoulders. On the bank of the river, we sit down. The two of us throw stones at the water. He opens a bag containing bread. Neither one of us eats. I inform him that I'm leaving.

My words shake him.

I then tell him that I can no longer continue to see don Victor. All the things he's done to me now appear magnified. The horror in Robertito's eyes doesn't stop me and I continue talking, with cadence, like the water that rushes below us. I also share with him my encounter with Manuel's friend. I ask him not to do anything, say I'm simply venting.

His hands caress my hair. His crying shakes his arms. But I don't remain silent, in spite of his tears. I tell him I need to be alone. He doesn't want to leave me. I insist. He moves away, enormous in size, turning to look back at me with each step.

The river. How much has it carried away? What used to be there, fresh and sparkling, trickling among the stones, nudging them to roll and sing? The river, young and healthy like the girls that saunter through the sown fields with their laughter. This river now green and sickly. This river that leaves the land bleak.

I didn't see Robertito on the way back. I'm not certain what's become of him. I'm still in San Juan and he's put distance between us.

In the station I wait for the bus. It's getting dark when I board. This time I'm not carrying any packages. My old dresses are tatters. The others I don't want. I'm wrapped in my mother's shawl. My empty hands are crossed on my lap.

Night's about to greet the dawn when I get off the bus.

I walk along the cobbled street. In the distance, the dim light of a tavern. Silence broken by the metallic clinking of glass. The door opens and a man comes out. He leaves the door ajar and a bevy of voices projects down the empty street.

He walks up to me teetering. I remain still. He places a hand on my shoulder. One eye is reddened. The other a sunken socket.

"Is it still today?" he asks.

I don't respond.

Other villagers peek out. Their silhouettes are dim and distant.

The man insists, with a pleading voice, "Is it still today?"

Releasing myself from the pressure of his hand, I begin to move away. As I turn the corner, I still hear him screaming.

"Please! Tell me! Is it still today!!"

Tide

In our house there are only women. The absence of men projects an enormous shadow on the wall. Among us, it's my grandmother's voice that resounds. Her words are spewed hoarsely. In each one there's a dark resentment that I'm not able to decipher.

I'm still not old enough to sit at the table. I eat on the floor, leaning against one of the appliances in the kitchen. The food slides awkwardly down my throat. It's a sticky paste, unable to be swallowed silently. Grandmother interrupts her chatter and screams at me for those sounds that I can't help but emit. She opens wide her mouth and I see a mouthful dissolving inside. I don't want to look at her, but she's prohibited me from taking my eyes off her while she's speaking to me.

In the afternoon, the sea becomes tinged with red. I watch the wind make the sand whirl. Along the coastline people button up their coats. The sun, already setting, strikes their faces and tinges them with an amber splendor. I peer out through the blinds covering the windows in the bathroom. Grandmother keeps the curtains closed.

"Otherwise, the tapestries will begin to fade," she explained the first time I attempted to open them.

In the dimly-lit living room she teaches me to knit. The yarn slips away from my hands. The knitting needles scratch me and turn my fingers red. At times I miss a stitch in the design. Grandmother snatches my work and undoes it until the place where I made the mistake. I'm not allowed to get up without finishing it. Upon my back there's a icy pain that never ceases. I'm sitting on the edge of the sofa. If I lean back, my elbows will rise and the knitting will be destroyed.

It's nighttime when I finish. Grandmother examines my work and permits me to go eat. In no time winter will arrive and she'll receive numerous requests for shawls and bedspreads. The wool wounds the fingers much less than thread does, but its stinging never goes away.

Outside it's black. I've never seen how night falls. So many nights in which I've felt its weight.

There are almost no summer vacationers. It's the end of March. Just like that day in March when she dropped me off at grandmother's. She. My mother's name is Andrea, but when I speak it, my grandmother changes it to She, as if she were speaking of an inanimate object. Or she reproaches me: *Your mother*, as if I had molded her with my own hands.

I must have been four years old; perhaps five, no more. I clung to her skirt and cried. Regardless, she left. The wind whipped her dress when she passed the garden gate. I was watching her long, candenced stride when my grandmother closed the front door. I wasn't able to glimpse her face. I don't even know if she turned around to see me with teary eyes or if she continued to walk to the rhythm of the wind. I just remember that her dress was yellow.

"You are not going to be like HER," my grandmother told me.

There two floors in the house. The bedrooms downstairs are occupied by the Claro women. Three daughters and their mother. She's as old as my grandmother but can no longer stand straight and her hands tremble. She wears a black shawl over black clothing and allows the days to slip away. Her voice cascades from her armchair . She barely opens her mouth, but the three daughters, who are no longer young, stop and observe. They remain immobilized, awaiting her words. The older woman gives an order and the three of them begin to move, in the same direction, with the same diligence. Their mother never thanks them; she merely emits sighs and complaints to the wind.

"She's been sick for years," my grandmother explains to me.

That's why no one can run or play in the patio adjacent to the windows. And the reason we have to ascend and descend the stairs on tiptoe.

The hardwood floors creak and we have to walk softly. If there's any sound whatsoever, one of the daughters asks alarmingly, "What's happening?" My grandmother grabs me by the arm and lifts me up, whispering, "Go ahead, make all the noise you can. What do you care if I lose my renters? What do you care? Just like Her. You both think you were born princesses and you never worry about all the sleepless nights anyone spends trying to help you get ahead, as if . . ."

I don't answer her. In the beginning, I tried to explain and my every word was merely an invitation to chastise me. I stand there motionless, in silence, listening to her and lowering my eyes when she compares me to my mother.

The woman in the kitchen is named Ema. My grandmother insists that among the two of us we can take care of the house without help. It's the Claro women that give us problems with their special dietary needs.

Ema stays until 3 p.m. The mornings are filled with her marvelous culinary scents. My favorite is the perfume of basil. I lay it upon the table and cut slender strips, then wipe my fingers on my arms, just to keep the aroma through the afternoon.

I take beans from the bag and I stretch each bean toward me until it splits in two. Once shelled, they fall into a pot of water. When it's full, I submerge my hands in it. It's like digging in wet sand on the rocky shore and finding stones the sea never swept away.

Ema works tethered to the stove. The heat envelops us; we open the window and take in the salty air. At times we turn on the radio. I love music, but I prefer to hear what the radio announcer has to say about what's beyond this window. It's as if the radio were sending me updates on my mother's movements.

Ema doesn't speak in complete sentences. She rarely lets a word slip. Always murmuring, as if in a hushed tone. I ask her if they speak in her home.

"The silly things you say!" she responds.

After lunch she leaves. She always wears the blue shawl that my grandmother knit. I see her advance a few meters. Slender, sylphlike, she hugs herself. Her steps are small and swift, almost sinuous. She unbraids her hair and lets it cascade down her back. She's young, just like the girls who came to summer here and have now departed.

On Tuesdays and Fridays we go to the cove on the coast. Grandmother leads the way. I almost have to run to keep up with her. Every so often she grabs my hand and yanks me to her hip.

"Don't be distracting yourself," she warns me. "They begin by leaving footprints and, in no time, all traces of them have vanished."

The sea's straight ahead, just a few meters. I feel the clamor of the waves and the wind. The sea foam surges and retreats. Each wave that approaches pelts itself, recedes, and then calls to the others. The sea's moaning paints a stark picture in the sand, one that absorbs and traps it like the airy stalks that capture the wind.

Grandmother knows the story of every type of fish. She opens them and reads what's inside. She examines their eyes, thrusts her fingers into their roseate entrails and then smells her fingers. She digs up clams and selects them, one by one. She begins filling the basket that I'm carrying.

At times, when we just arrive and she's in a favorable mood, she allows me to run in the sand along the shore near the boats. I carry my shoes in one hand and with the other, I draw traces in the air that the wind gradually whisks away. My knees give way to the warm sand. Some seagulls approach me from the sea. They don't advance too closely, nor do I attempt to close in on them. I gather their dampened feathers and lick and savor the salty spatter. Grandmother calls me and makes me discard them.

The basket keeps getting heavier. On the way home I switch the arm that carries it. In the distance, the sea is never silent.

In our house the furniture is all wooden. On top of each table is portrait of my grandmother's son. He was a dark, slender young man. In every picture he's serious. And in not one of the photos is he looking at the camera.

"My Pedro," my grandmother bemoans. "Indeed, he would've been a fine gentleman." Or, "If the good seed sown doesn't survive, all that's left are weeds."

Some fifteen years ago, the sea swallowed him. He was seeking shellfish from a rock when the waves overcame him. The others managed to run away, but he didn't notice. He heard their shouts to get out too late. All that remained on the rock were gleaming water and silence. They never found him.

"The sea's deceiving," she tells me.

I'd like to take my chances. To let the white foam envelop me and allow my skin to be soaked with its scents. To feel the striking of the furious waves against my legs. To feel it's cool freshness upon my belly. To let the force of the wave take me far from shore, so far away that I no longer hear the seagulls and the beached boats are merely colorful dots along the shore.

"Don't let me catch you getting too close to the sea," Grandmother warns me.

There are times I want to protest: "Everyone gets to bathe in the ocean."

"Just do what everyone else does and let's see what happens. Besides, no one needs to get soaked in salt water. Find something else to complain about."

But the sea's still there and never ceases to sing.

It's time for me to attend school. Along the way, our backs are turned to the sea. The church is in front of the plaza. Our classes are held either behind the church or in the back patio.

The director takes me to a classroom while my grandmother reminds me to be courteous and well-behaved.

"Here we like our girls to be obedient and respectful. They come here to study and learn to be proper young ladies. To live by the mandates of the Lord and not offend Him with our failings. You wouldn't want Him to be saddened by transgressions, isn't that right?"

I assure her that I'm totally in agreement with a shaking of my head. She asks me how many prayers I know, what I like to do for entertainment, and how I help around the house. Grandmother has already taught me the right answers, and I repeat them in a soft voice.

In the office, the director asks my grandmother to fill out some forms. They speak. I'm hoping that some young girl enters, as I still don't know anyone my age. I'm not certain how I should respond. I've seen the girls playing in the sand. It seems so easy for every one of them to slip in and out the sea, calling out to other girls, moving away from the shore and approaching the sand and the foam.

Grandmother buys me the reading and spelling books, the Bible, notebooks, a black pen, an eraser, and a box of colored pencils.

In the kitchen she teaches me how to sharpen my pencils with a knife. We use brown paper to cover the books. Grandmother writes my name on the cover of each one. Large, twisting letters that bind me.

She also puts my name on my apron, which she embroiders with red thread to match the ribbons in my hair. She won't be buying me shoes until winter, so I'll be wearing the white ones. I'm terrified at the thought of being different from the others. The young girls I used to see from my window no longer appear. I ask Grandmother if the schoolgirls are like the ones that summer at the sea.

"Whether they're like the girls on summer vacation is none of your business. All you have to worry about is doing what I tell you to do and learning from the classes you're taught. I've spent plenty and if you're not going to take advantage of this opportunity, that's it. If you're not going to take advantage of it, you'll just remain at home. There's a lot to do here."

All the girls have bathed in the sea. The teacher asks us how we spent our vacation. Some went to the countryside, others traveled to distant beaches, some simply stayed here. But each and every one of them had bathed in the sea. They just say it outright. They've been moved by a certain land-scape or a certain experience, but the sea is ever present. Their skin and the waves have met so many times they even don't bother to turn around to glimpse the water or search for it in the darkness of night.

During recess, a girl with braids tells me, "I bet that you've never been in the sea. That's why you asked so many questions."

"Impossible!" another girl intervenes. "She surely has bathed in the sea."

"Perhaps not. There are people who won't get in the water, like my aunt."

"They may not always go into the water, but, of course, they've bathed in the sea. Everyone has done it."

"Well, have you bathed in the sea?"

I want to say no so they'll keep telling me stories about it. But I know this would make me different and I respond in the affirmative.

"Just a few times. My grandmother isn't fond of the sea, so I rarely go and hardly know how to swim."

"Didn't I tell you! Everyone has experienced the sea!"

"Not everyone." The girl with the braids looks at me with disgust.

"Of course, the sea's everywhere."

"In the countryside there's no sea and the peasants have never seen it."

"Maybe not there, but around here . . ."

They move away chattering among themselves. They aren't interested in me. Many of these girls have known each other for a while. They play together in groups. I run after them to watch what they're doing. They don't invite me. I'm fine with that. I don't know what to do, and they seem to know that.

The teacher gives us assignments. I have lunch in the kitchen with Ema and help her serve dessert to the Claro women. We clear the table and I sit down to do my homework. Grandmother corrects my handwriting. The pages turn gray from all the erasing. The rubber eraser has grown small and crumbles. Grandmother continues to erase.

"Until it's perfect."

My completed homework assignments are handsome. The teacher shows the other girls my work. Then she asks me to read the lessons. I repeat them until I know them by heart. Then I continue to repeat them because my intonation isn't quite right. Bread is baking in the kitchen. I remove my things and we set the table for tea. Mrs. Adriana sits in the chair with arms and cushions. Placed in front of her is a row of colored pills. The teacup trembles in her hands. All around her the tablecloth becomes stained. Each pill is accompanied by a groan.

"What enslavement, Holy Father!"

Her daughters watch her. They always watch her, like cats on the prowl. They strain their necks forward, their hands barely touching the table, ready to stand up and race to their mother's side.

I leave with the bread basket and I return with it brimming with bread. Only white bread, without the crust. Transparent slices of sweetened quince. The honey slightly warmed. Slices of fresh cheese without salt. Sometimes an apricot marmalade made by the oldest of the daughters, tasted by the second daughter before serving it.

"We found mold one time."

"Your carelessness almost cost me my life," the elderly woman sighs.

"Don't say such a thing, Mother. It gave us quite a fright."

They talk about some relatives. They read letters that they send and receive. They recall the faults of each family member. They're pretentious and full of pride and rarely visit the women, just some people from Santiago and the most distinguished individuals in the area; people that would barely take notice of my grandmother.

I snack on the bread they leave. It's so soft that it melts on my tongue before I can even swallow it.

It's a warm afternoon. Grandmother has a fever and is staying in bed. "You know very well what you have to do. Go downstairs," she instructs me.

Her voice sounds weary. Harsher and, at the same time, more gentle. Her bedroom has a smell that isn't hers. Redolent and portentous, it envelops the walls and penetrates the center of the room where I'm standing. The curtains are drawn. There's a lamp lit on the nightstand, but the tilted shade barely allows even a sliver of light to slip out. In the semi-darkness she appears much smaller. Between the white sheets she's even more pale. I hadn't realized how much she's aged.

I organize my notebooks and begin my assignments. The kitchen door behind me is open. Ema is about to finish cleaning and leave. The eldest of the Claro daughters checks to see if their part of the house has been put in order. Her name is Marta. She moves about slowly. She speaks in a soft voice, almost dragging her words. Everything about her is measured and methodical. Even her smile barely stretches between her chubby cheeks, where it remains, softening her features and giving her a youthfulness she no longer has.

"How's your grandmother doing?" she ask me.

I turn and tell her that I don't know. I return to my books and hear her murmuring with Ema. An uncomfortable, imprecise fear begins to cloud the pages. Grandmother has always been there. That's why they brought me to live with her. If she gets sick, they won't know where to take me.

There are no erasures on the pages of my homework this afternoon.

I sit in the armchair and knit. With the curtains wide open. There beyond is the sea. An expanse of azure that opens itself to the sun. Behind the clouds, the sun slowly begins to set, as if in the descent it might find the pleasure of submerging itself in the profound depths of this vast body of water.

Marta calls me into the kitchen. "Take this tray to your dear grandmother. I prepared her a cup of linden tea and a bowl of my mother's consomme. Ask her if she needs anything else."

I carry the tray carefully up the stairs. I have the feeling that I'm going to fall and I slow down. Grandmother's bedroom is dark. The lamp next to bed on the nightstand is no longer lit. I approach the bulging form of her body. Her heavy snoring creates a harsh wind that would wrest the deepest of roots.

I stand there holding the tray. I speak to her and she doesn't respond. I should touch her and gently nudge, but I'm unable. The only table in the room is covered with trinkets, so I have nowhere to place the tray that's becoming heavy in my hands. I call out to her in a louder voice. She doesn't awaken.

"Your food's going to get cold!" I shout in the tone of a whisper.

If I went back downstairs holding the tray in front of me, I wouldn't be able to see my feet and would end up falling. I don't know what else to say, so I begin humming. Her snoring remains rhythmical. I raise a leg and stretch it out toward her body, to nudge her with my heel. When I'm about to touch her, I lose my balance and fall to the side. The contents on the tray clatter to the floor. Through the strands of my hair I see how the linden tea and consommé have fused into a steaming and watery pool of green. My raised leg has struck my grandmother, who sits straight up. I crouch down to pick up the pieces. The napkin is soaked and the liquid is still there, glimmering in the light of the lamp that Grandmother has just switched on.

"Don't stand there looking dazed. Run and get the mop!"

While I'm cleaning, she doesn't stop talking. She tells me how to mop the floor, to not make any noise, and how much she regrets the loss of such fine china, which was broken by the carelessness of someone who doesn't value anything because she hasn't earned anything.

"Just like Her!" she insists as I leave.

I return to the kitchen and prepare tea and toast. The door to the Claro's part of the house is closed and I don't dare ask them for help, so I take my grandmother the only thing I know how to prepare. I keep her company while she stirs and sips her tea. She isn't quite totally sitting up. The pillows seem to close in around her, barely leaving a narrow space in which she fits snugly. The wooden floor upon which I stand is still sticky. The soles of my white shoes launch a strident complaint with each of my movements, so I try to stay still while I watch her.

She barely touches the toast. She tells me to take away the tray. She falls back among the pillows and breathes deeply. I leave her enveloped in a thick, heavy semi-darkness.

In the living room, someone has drawn the curtains. I sit down to knit. Among the windowpanes, the splendor of the sun dazzles as it dives into the sea.

Grandmother is still sick.

Ema stays until the Claro women have had their tea. The elderly woman tells me that I may join them at the table while they are taking tea. Emphasizing *while they are taking tea.*

At the table I try not to make any sounds and don't take a bite of anything. Marta is the one who eats the most toast. She cuts slices and slathers them with butter or marmalade. She puts entire pieces delicately into her mouth. Her jaws grind them in a matter of minutes and, in no time, she's prepared another bite.

The second eldest daughter of the Claros is Josefa. She is thin and almost never eats. Her nose is aquiline, like that of her sister, but it's placed in a face that's much more slender and gaunt. Her eyes remain fixed on everything, her head erect upon her bony shoulders, and the line of her mouth taut with tension.

Lidia is the youngest of the three. When they're all together, it's notable that she's much younger than the others. Given her tied back hair, her dark clothing and shawls, I thought she was just like her sisters. Her skin is still translucent, and in her eyes there's a gleam that the other two have lost. Or never had. She moves her hands ably. Her lips are crimson and vibrant. She looks at me and smiles. She takes the bread basket and offers me toast. The others don't even realize that I've openly taken a sip of tea.

I leave the table and Ema washes the dishes. On the counter there's a tray for my grandmother. She shows me the pot on the stove that I should heat up later.

Someone has drawn the curtains before I sit down to knit. I already finished some pieces and have more to do. The same color, the same shape. They'll start accumulating if Grandmother doesn't improve.

Another afternoon. I complete my homework without an erasure. Lidia approaches me from behind.

"Do you want me to help you?"

I don't need help, I'm almost done. I thank her. She stays there observing me. She asks me about school, the other girls, my lessons. She makes me read a passage. She strokes my hair and says I'm very dear. That's what they say to the girls who aren't so pretty.

"I, too, was diligent and dedicated like you. I've saved many of my diplomas."

I ask her to show them to me, but her mother is sleeping now and she can't enter the room to look for them.

"I even have a medal," she smiles. "Golden, with a tri-colored ribbon. Perhaps I could lend it to you."

I imagine the faces of the girls in my class if were to arrive to school with a medal hanging from my neck and hiding the radiant medal behind my checkered apron.

Lidia tells me, "Tomorrow."

In the evening, Grandmother again returns the tray of food untouched. She doesn't even scold me. There's an uncertain odor in her room. The shadows shade moans that are unheard.

Marta and Josefa go upstairs, their footsteps resounding. They tell me they're worried about the sound coming from my grandmother's chest. They're going to call their mother's physician.

"Don't worry, child. It surely isn't anything serious."

Marta makes a vague gesture, as if she were stroking my scalp. But it disappears before reaching me.

Upon leaving school, there's Lidia. She's carrying a bag of folded linens under her arm. She clings tightly to a purse.

"Would you like to accompany me while I shop and run some errands?"

She's happy. She doesn't get out much. Church functions, Sunday mass, and returning to the store. We trapaise along a path of dried leaves that moan under our steps and disintegrate. The bag begins to swell after every stop. Lidia hangs on to the receipts. I ask her why she keeps them.

She explains that her mother controls all the expenses. She jots them down in a notebook. She receives a pension as a widow and payment for a rental in the center of Santiago. She's saving in the event that she has a major illness.

"She doesn't want to end up dying in a typical ward in the local hospital."

We shop for fabrics in the store. Lidia and her sisters sew only what they need. I tell her to create a blouse with a colorful pattern. She holds the different fabrics up and examines herself in the mirror.

The wind's still warm. Her bun becomes undone a bit. Her skin is tinted with several shades of color. She resembles the summer vacationers. Even though she may be very different.

The doctor arrives before lunch. The Claro sisters accompany him. He tells them about the infection in her lungs, the treatments, the x-rays. He charges them and they're the ones who bring the boxes containing the pills upstairs. They speak with Grandmother and leave her the pills. I merely go upstairs with a glass of water.

"The fortune all this is going to cost!" she complains, collapsing between the pillows.

"You should eat something," Marta tells her. "Tomorrow you have to have some x-rays taken at the hospital. You won't be able to walk if you don't have the energy."

Grandmother eats something.

She takes her pills.

She determines the cost of everything.

The Claro sisters talk in their room. I'm outside the door and hear everything. I'm there because I don't have to be anywhere at that moment. Their mother, Adriana, sighs. Among her groans, she insists that one of her daughters should accompany my grandmother.

"She can go with Ema, can't she?" Josefa intercedes.

"She can. She can go accompanied by an illiterate and a child, and she can collapse along the way and die. It's not that I want for any of you to have to go, but here we have a problem of conscience."

Josefa doesn't want to go because it's the day she attends meetings at the church. Marta suffers from an ongoing pain in her waist, which is intensified in autumn. Their mother, Adriana, isn't fond of the idea of Lidia going alone. She's still young and they can take advantage of her naivete. But finally she agrees that Lidia should be the one.

Grandmother's much smaller. She doubles over at the waist. A hoarse moan shudders through her back. Wrapped in a shawl she descends the stairs. Short, slight, heavy steps.

"You should be in class. I don't know where you came up with the whimsical idea to stay at home today. The world out there. That's what you want. Just like Her, the world."

90

Lidia smiles at me above Grandmother's inclined head.

While riding in the bus, she falls asleep. She doesn't say a single word. She sways from side to side with each turn in the road.

"Are you familiar with the port?" I ask Lidia.

She tells me that she's been there twice. It's been awhile. They're accustomed to going together and now that their mother, Adriana, is weak with a heart condition, it's become more difficult.

At times the road veers away from the sea, but then it draws near again and grazes the suspended rocks. It's as if it wanted to fling itself onto the dampened rocks and wind among the sea's white traces.

Grandmother's eyelids are closed. A white line is formed where her eyes shut. She has almost no eyelashes. The brows shadow the mass of her forehead.

"The sea looks different from the port," Lidia adds.

The waves never reach the port to break upon the shore. Stone breakwalls trap them. So much impetus in the shadows of faded sheds. The surface is dark as the darkest green among the hills. An opaque reflection of a sky darkened with shades of gray. A liberated song silenced by voices that spill onto the still water. The murmur of boats grazing each other while asleep.

"They're all so different. So many different sizes, they're so compressed," I observe, leaning on the glass window.

The hospital's at the top of a large hill, facing the sea. It's a large, white building inclined toward the steps people climb to enter the building. Grandmother leans on my shoulder and hangs onto Lidia's arm. Her breathing is labored. She has to stop after a couple of steps. She raises her eyes toward the still-distant door. Her large pupils are dilated. Halfway there. The neglected garden is filled with yellow flowers with very few petals. They're returning to the soil.

The wait is very long. She trembles on the gurney. There in the distance are the machines.

"The young girl cannot go into the x-ray room," insists a man.

He's dressed in white, but he isn't a doctor. Even though he's young, he appears exhausted. He smiles at Lidia and speaks as if he's apologizing.

"Hospital orders."

It's a long wait in the hallway. Almost nobody looks at me. Through the windows one can see the sea wedged within the port. A tamed sea that neither bellows nor bucks, but from the depths of itself escapes the swells that are now her voice and strike incessantly at the walls and the windows.

Lidia walks away, clinging to the bag with both hands. Behind her is Grandmother, stretched out on the hospital gurney, covered with a green sheet. All of her belongings are there by her feet. Her face appears like a dried out walnut among the the folds of the fabric.

A man in white is pushing the gurney. He moves swiftly and I have to run behind Lidia. Lidia speaks to him in a hushed voice. When he responds to her, the speed diminishes. It's then when I finally reach them. He again begins to move swiftly and I have to pick up the pace. Finally I reach them. He hurries again and I struggle to keep up with them. The tiles are cold and the green and white pattern never ends, nor does the gurney stop rolling. Outside, the sea is imprisoned.

We have to leave Grandmother at the hospital. It's a large room, with beds placed side by side from the door to the closed window. She's placed toward the end, next to the cloudy glass window that separates us from the sea. Each of the sick patients is hidden in a green rectangle. The folds in the sheets are like the sea. A half-washed sea in which their moans are lost. Almost all of them are alone.

"What are you doing here wasting time? Perhaps they closed the school?"

Her voice is faded and her chest trembles. Lidia comes for me and Grandmother attempts to apologize.

"What an inconvenience to make you come all the way here, Miss Lidia! My granddaughter's whims, there's no reason for this..." and she struggles a bit more to offer explanations. I tell her that I'm attending school every morning and that Lidia likes to get out.

Why should I tell her that Lydia went to the cafeteria and conversed with the young man that pushed the gurney? They stirred their tea until it cooled, looked longingly at one another, and spoke in hushed voices. A couple of afternoons later, I'll see that they no longer just touch legs but rather are drawn to and hug one another, and their hands, beneath the table, seek, squeeze and grope the other's.

I stay longer with grandmother. I do my homework and she naps, coughing all the time. I then knit a bit. They bring her food early in the day and I feed her. Soup with semolina, puree, jello. Everything lukewarm and

92

tasteless, she complains between bites. I smile because I think she isn't going to die. The sea's dark outside the cloudy window. But you hear it roar in the afternoon near sunset.

We return by bus before nightfall. I thank Lidia over and over again, as my grandmother instructed me. She says, "I should be grateful to her that she became sick. If not, how would I have ever met Manuel?"

She ties her thick dark hair back into a ponytail that cascades over her shoulders like water among rocks, and remains quiet, melancholic. She wipes the makeup from her face and smiles at me:

"You aren't going to say a thing to anyone, correct?"

"I don't have anything to tell them," I respond.

Lidia tells me that he studies in the evening and wants to progress. That he's only going to be in the port for a short time, until he obtains his degree for teaching middle school and can go to Santiago to continue studying. He wants to be a physician's assistant or something like that. I ask her why her mother doesn't allow her to marry.

"It's not that she doesn't allow me. It's just that the four of us have always been together and united and not one of us has ever thought about leaving. At least not while our mother is alive. But this is different. Manuel would never accept it. He's from another class and it's something I can't explain to you because you wouldn't understand."

That's how Lidia spoke the first several days. Now she's silent. I see the anguish in her eyes. When they inform us that Grandmother is better and can return home on the weekend, she makes the journey, crying all the way. She pretends to read a book. I see that the page never turns and she wipes her eyes every so often

I take her hand and tell her, "I can help you so you can continue to see him."

Although I have no idea as to how to go about it.

We take Grandmother home in a taxi.

"To whom but the princess would it occur to spend this enormously useless amount of money," she complains before getting in. The breeze from the sea envelops her and she collapses upon the seat panting. Her hands tremble and she cannot keep her eyes open.

Manuel accompanies us to the door and helps her get comfortable. He and Lydia stay there holding hands, speaking softly, leaning into one another, as if they wanted to surpass their flesh and submerge themselves in a sea of warm and torrential blood.

I sit in the back next to grandmother. I adjust her shawl and watch how the drizzle dissipates on the steed of steel, erect and forceful in its twisting of an imprisioned beast.

At home, Grandmother gets up for awhile in the morning and goes to bed after lunch.

"When it comes to more effort, the strength is there."

I see her undress while I'm reciting my lesson. Her body is small and spent, like a dry branch of eucalyptus. Her bare chest rubs between two breasts that cave in to her abdomen. The skin of her legs resembles sand traversed by birds. She wraps herself in a white nightshirt and a bed jacket that she herself knit. I think that maybe my mother is starting to resemble my grandmother. She's always youthful in my memory, but time has to also be residing within her body.

"How old is my mother?" I ask.

"Old enough to distinguish what's right from what's wrong."

"And how old are you?"

"Older than I would like to be."

"Do you think that Miss Lidia is still young enough to get married?"

"One is always young enough to do foolish things, right? And enough of your questions. Pass me your notebook so I can see what blunders you've made while I was gone."

Afterward I go to the kitchen and help as best I can, even though Josefa is in charge of preparing the tea. Sometimes Lidia tells me to ask her for help and we go out together shopping or to look for a book from the church or whatever it occurs to her to suggest to me. We run on the cool sand of the beach toward the white silhouette of Manuel. Lidia's medal bounces off my chest as I jump among the sea foam and the sand dampened by the dark sea of winter. They come and go, sneaking away among the distant rocks and speaking so softly that their words don't cut through the wind.

Later we approach the plaza and I finally do what we pretended we were going to do. They lag behind and wait for me, delaying the farewell, pulling apart from one another slowly and painfully. He walks to the bus stop in the opposite direction. He stays there waiting, becoming small and fragile.

94

We walk without looking back or waving our hands until we arrive at the curve and can longer see him. Then we tighten our jackets energetically and Lidia remarks that this winter is especially cold, or that my grandmother already seems better, or that this evening she's going to prepare something special to eat, and finally, next to the fence, she thanks me.

The wind never ceases to be bone-chilling and penetrating when the sun begins to intertwine with the air and the first pines begin to turn green. The sea dissolves the gray layer of mist, elevates its brilliant waters and gathers from the sky white brushstrokes which have turned transparent.

In the sand, birds leave new traces that become entangled with those of the previous visitors from the weekend. The hushed afternoons are broken by children's voices as they play along the beach and draw near the sea without touching it. Couples stroll arm in arm along the path of water and sand, and amidst the boardwalk several shops open like enormous mouths that calls out to passersby to gather in the afternoons and to linger in the evenings.

I've told Lidia that I want to bathe in the sea. That I need to soak myself in salt water and feel the furious force of the waves against my skin. That I so long to stand there on the wet sand, awaiting the attack of the writhing water. That I'm going to scream so loudly that one won't even hear the moans of the sea nor the howls of the wind. That I'm going to fall backwards, then sideways, every which way, while sea foam gently passes over my body and covers it with its white sheets.

"As soon as the weather gets better, I'll take you to the beach and we'll bathe in the sea," Lidia promises me.

In the afternoons, for a while, I put my knitting aside, I open the door to the street and peer out. I feel the wind against my face, each day a bit warmer, each day less restless, each day, closer.

"The immense sea at times appears tiny to soothe the anxiety of seeing it come and go, but it's always there in front of me like a green and white wall. . ." That's what Lidia seems to murmur along the sidewalk on the bridge. She's carrying a bag in each hand to balance the weight. It's a slow, rhythmic swaying. The hem of her dress flutters. The wind has no rhythm. The figures traced by her skirt are capricious. Her hair, captured in a bun, doesn't move.

In the window, Josefa. A perpendicular figure in opposition to the horizontal figure of the sea. Eyes that pierce like crystals and writhe in that body that Lidia continues to make sway to the rhythm of the sea.

It's such a brief movement that Josefa makes to cross the street to meet up with us. Lidia and Manuel are embracing. I'm eating an ice cream. It's an afternoon like all the others, but Josefa happened to appear at the corner. She continued to follow us and turned around to pretend that the encounter was unplanned. She stands there, watching their arms became un-entwined. Her eyes never divert from lips now ghostly white, shoulders that are bent forward, from eyelids extended in a line parallel to the ground that absorbs the new silence.

"It's best that you come with me, wouldn't you agree?" she says.

Lidia moves away and runs toward her sister. On the way home, she doesn't stop speaking. It's a murmur that implores and beseeches. I'm unable to distinguish her words, but I understand Josefa's silences.

At home, they enter their mother's bedroom and close the door. Grand-mother sees that Lidia is crying and asks me why. It doesn't make any sense for me to remain silent so I tell her everything. I think she's going to feel bad for her, but instead, she grabs my arm forcefully and takes me up the stairs.

"How lovely!" she mumbles. "What a wonderful attitude! It couldn't have occurred to you to do anything more appropriate or proper than to serve as a go-between? And now, just how am I going to look Mrs. Adriana in the face? How am I going to explain to her that a twisted tree produces rotten fruit? All that I've done for you to make you a decent person and look at how you respond to all my efforts! Not even She would have come up with such a scheme. And even less so at your age. At least she began to stray when she was a bit older. The little brat searching for liaisons for decent people!"

"I didn't do anything. I just accompanied her to go for walks and such."

"And to meet up with a man! Don't you see what this kind of person is like, that they raise suspicions even less than an average good-for-nothing."

"He's very nice and she likes to be with him, and here they don't let her do anything. And I want to see a bride in the church."

"From now on, you won't step foot outside other than to go to school. And don't show your face to Mrs. Adriana until I tell you how things stand. Grab your knitting and get comfortable, because you won't be moving from here."

The days drag on. I no longer help in the kitchen nor do I sit in the living room in the afternoons. Night tarries in arriving. Against the glass of the window I feel the warm air that must slightly graze the sea, covering it

96

with a thin, warm layer that later opens up to the bodies that penetrate the black abyss of its green waters.

One morning, Lidia comes to my bed. She tells me hurriedly that she's leaving. An aunt of Manuel's is going to take them in. That she's going to have to venture out and search for a job. From there they'll see how things are going. She's full of sadness for her mother, who no longer speaks to her and rejects her. And she doesn't even know that Lidia is leaving. How will she react when she finds out?

"She says that I'm no longer her daughter."

She must have said something else. I heard the screams and the silence. And I've seen the weight her shoulders bear.

She's trembling and appears very thin. Her eyes are desperate, similar to those of a frightened dog. That's fear. The air is far too vast beyond the house. There are too many winding paths from this door to others. Lidia's hands and skin are numb with fear.

Grandmother tells me that Lidia left a letter and fled. She took a small suitcase and walked along the sidewalk, leaning against the walls as if she were searching for a firm arm to help her continue walking along.

The sun's high overhead. The shellfish catchers arrive early and fan out across the sand. Some of them dive into the water—for just a short while and only in the surf, but there they are, in the white and green foam.

The nights fall into a deep and dark silence, enveloped by a sea that roars, embracing its blackness, and murmurs in a whisper secret words. It's difficult for me to sleep. Through the window the immense stain of the sea at night is now like the mouth of an abyss that chafes with the wind. The chilly air swirls around with its scents and sneaks into my room through the open window. Everything seems still outside, but I know that they're running their hands over each other and delighting in each caress of every night.

The hinge of a door squeaks. One of the floorboards creaks. A piece of fabric rustles gently. I descend the stairs without making a sound.

Josefa is on the large sofa. She's face down on the cushions. Her white nightshirt is drawn up around her waist and her exposed legs, thin and restless, open and close, twisting like sea foam. One hand is lost between them and the other around her neck. Her movements are so convulsive and her moans so profound that I want to approach her to see her face. But I remain motionless, hidden in the darkness, listening to how her body placates itself and lies still after the stifled scream among the tapestries.

She stands up, arranges herself, and buttons her nightshirt. She then sits down and looks toward where I am, though she doesn't see me. She tosses her head back and flings her hair over her shoulders. In her large, strong hands, the veins are thick and prominent. She moans and asks why not her, and continues to murmur words I don't understand. Her chest begins to stop shaking and the strain in her hands relaxes. When she walks back to her room, she passes right by me. She's soaked in sweat and tears.

Upon awakening, we find Doña Adriana dead. She, who had so many pains and illnesses, didn't die of just one thing during her sleep. More like everything together. I'm preparing to go to school when we hear Marta's scream. Josefa runs to find the doctor. I peek in the door and see that she's blue, stretched out upon the bed among the white sheets and pillows. Her mouth is white and violet. The curtains are drawn and the air is heavy.

Grandmother enters and begins to examine her. Even though from the very first moment she knows she's not breathing, she remains there for some time, touching her and searching for some form of life. Marta begins to pray and I think it's going to be impossible for me to go to school, so I stand next to her and repeat the litany. Grandmother brings a chair and a tea for Marta. She hands me a rosary and sits down next to us, her head bent forward and her voice weary. I imagine that she's going over the bills, thinking that the renters are going to leave her and that she won't be able to keep the house.

Ema arrives before the doctor and also accompanies us in prayer. She appears deathly pale when he arrives.

Josefa says to me, "Go search for Father Alfonso and run to the home of Doña Elvira and tell her what's happened so she can inform the others. I'm going to the port to make arrangements with the funeral home."

I'm leaving when I hear Marta say to her, "Call Lidia."

"Later," she replies.

Grandmother and Marta bathe and dress the woman. The coffin arrives and they place it in the dining room, on top of the table. The men move the body. I remain in the empty room that now has a distinct odor. Some women arrive, bringing flowers, and a never ending prayer begins.

It's growing dark when I hears Lidia's heels clicking as she runs along the sidewalk. I'm about to open the door for her, but Josefa steps in front of me.

"You killed her!" she tells her.

Seated next to the enormous black box, Lidia cannot control her tears.

Before summer arrives and the earth that covers doña Adriana hardens, my mother appears. She draws back the curtains. She fills the house with her perfume and a voice I didn't remember. Her elegant hand with manicured nails takes my hand and we go out. I walk along to the rhythm of the jingling of her bracelets. A gentleman awaits us. The car he's driving rapidly leaves the sea behind.

My mother is now married and is an elegant and respected woman. She has had two small children. We spend the summer together. We've gone to the countryside and to a lake. I've swum in still waters. I sink slowly and only when my head surfaces, do I stretch out upon the water and float for hours. The sun casts its rays upon my face. At times I go underwater and savor the water, expecting it to be salty and stout, like the seawater. My little brothers splash about along the shore. I take them in my arms and carry them to the transparent chasm where I dry them off with a towel. They whine while clinging to my neck.

One afternoon Grandmother dies. She'd been sick for months and we never visited her. Not for months or years. The coffin is sealed when my mother and I enter the chapel. In the silence of the nave of the church, the elderly, unaccompanied women maintain a harsh yet still murmur. Ema's on one side of my grandmother. She hugs herself, crossing the lapels of her jacket that perhaps is still the very same one from before.

It's dark. It takes a while for me to distinguish the Claro sisters. One elderly and two older women. For a moment, I think that Lidia isn't there, that finally she's gone away, and that it's just her two sisters taking care of her sick mother. I approach them to greet them or perhaps they approach us. Marta is hunched over and her hands tremble. She says she hasn't been well because of an illness she names but that I don't recognize. Her smile is oblique and the thick skin of her face sags. Josefa sustains her firmly. On the other side, Lidia bends toward her and guides her diligently. Her hair is opaque, streaked with white. Her skin has become ashen, her eyes, blurry. I should ask, but I don't say a word. I don't want to hear her answer.

When we leave the cemetery, I tell my mother that I've never bathed in the sea. That I'd love for us to walk to the beach so I could run among the waves, perhaps with our clothing on or even without it, so that this will be the afternoon that I lose myself in the green and turbulent water.

Her response is, "Not now." She has to attend to some matters regarding the sale of Grandmother's house. The Claro sisters are going to buy it. "Besides, it's cold and the gusts of wind make the skin tighten."

"There'll be other opportunities," she replies.

And with the certainty of someone who's lost herself in the sea innumerable times, she adds, "Many."

Fatigued Material

"Take me back to the sea," she began. "I need to go back to the sea," she muttered while tugging at the lapels of the vest on the man she had in front of her. Soon she began to scream at us: "I told you to take me to the sea! For once in your lives, obey my orders!" In other moments she drew near us sweetly and between funny faces and complaints tried to convince us. "The sea's so beautiful. You're going to love it. When we're there I'm going to invite you to eat shellfish near the beach," and she described some hotel that perhaps existed or was only a mere lie to convince us. The majority of the time, she simply cried by the window and murmured crestfallen: "I'll never return to the sea. I'll never get out of here."

The hills overcame her. Harsh green waterfalls, gusts of banished wind. Before we'd see her climbing happily among the hills, staying at the crest to fill her lungs with the cold wind, turning her back on the imaginary sea, forgetting for years the torrential waters. She'd run along the slopes and laugh among the grasses. Down below, the city rising, cupolas of cement slithering up and along the slope, and she still higher, in the wind, her breathing both anxious and cheerful.

Now, having forgotten the meadows, she continued, "I need to return to the sea. Take me back to the sea."

Slices of bread with butter, a layer of jam. I sandwich them together and wrap it in a paper napkin. I put it in a bag. I finish drinking a lukewarm tea and head out the door.

It's just a little past six o'clock in the morning and already there's a line at the bus stop.

"It's cold," someone says.

Nobody responds. Someone is distracted and barely nods in agreement. No one is interested in conversing or acknowledging one another. Immobilized in their own irritability, in that accumulated tedium that pushes them from their beds every day. For months I've been sleeping on a bed I create every night with blankets and cushions in the dining room of my home, immersed in the odor of mildew in the dense wool. The odor often reappears in someone's jacket or in a bathroom towel. At any given moment a whiff revives my resentment toward my father, who's spellbound by that woman and chasing his own children away. My brothers scatter. I don't. I stay there to ruin their honeymoon, so my opaque gaze can extend across the room and cast a shadow on the festive lights of their party.

But everyone respects boundaries, whatever their night was like, whatever happened behind closed doors. Wasn't it like that in my family? We had the thickest door, the highest windows, and the patio with the bright-colored roses. And inside, blankets on the floor, screams, the violence of closed fists and repressed rage.

I find a seat on the bus and try to read the photocopies. We leave behind wide streets and paths with emaciated trees. The bus enters the highway and passes beneath recently constructed bridges.

I entered the house and saw her from behind, leaning over the sink. The faucet was open and water was running, wasted needlessly. I often found her that way, caught between the kitchen and the unmade beds of her children.

"This is runoff water," she'd say. "Water from the mountain," she'd clarify. "Or is it from a well?" she'd ask teary-eyed. "And the water from the sea, why doesn't it arrive?" she'd ask. "Water from the pipes comes with who knows how much filth?" she'd protest, her teeth clenched tightly. "If I could have just a little bit of salty water until you take me back there, a little of the special water that leaves my skin so white and firm. That water softens me, loosens my skin. Look at my hands! These aren't my hands. Give me back my hands."

And with hands that had become foreign to her, she'd pound the

102

walls and furniture until she was bleeding. She broke cups and plates. "You take me back there or I'll break everything." Afterwards, the loud noise against the floor.

No-one could live like that.

"It's not her speaking," the doctor had said. "It's the tumor." A large cyst which couldn't be stopped or removed, it was going to take over her body.

My father said, "Words are one thing. They can be tolerated. But the violence is another. That simply cannot be." So he tied her to the bed. We loosened the ties so she could go to the bathroom, so that she walked a bit, to silence her furious screams.

"You'll see, you'll see. I'm not going to take you with me. And if you dare to follow me, I am going to bury your head in the sand, I'm going to choke you in the sea. The fish will eat you, dismember you. They bite, you know. They bite and tear you into pieces, they devour the drowned. That's why they never find them. The fish open their huge mouths and chew them up before they become blue and wrinkled."

At nightfall he gagged her. "I can't live like this," he told us again. And he sat down at the table and we ate. It was difficult for us to talk over the beating of her tied feet and arms, the shaking of the bed. We made noise with the silverware and spoke about how the food that day was especially tasty. One of my brothers brought a television to the head of the dining table and left it there, always turned on, deafening the hoarse battering from the room of our mother.

They couldn't last. Neither the tumor nor she. They tried to devour one another until the only thing that remained was a convulsive body and confused words that were no longer threatening but rather incoherent screams. The night before part of her body became paralyzed and she was left hunched and twisted, we heard our father collapse on top of her. Even though he could no longer stand her, he never abandoned the habit of getting in bed with her before going to sleep, of grabbing her violently and harshly, of shaking his immense body and choking her when he crashed on top of what was left of his wife.

On a morning program a psychologist speaks about family constellations. "You have to spread our family out like a constellation to understand your history. Make a sketch of the lines between everyone."

While I listen, I begin to draw.

"Not only those that are closest, but also those individuals who have influenced you and have been a permanent presence in your life," she clarifies to the attentive and invisible listeners.

Whirling above the paper are the names of my father, distant and serious, his aggressive, harsh gaze. And those of my brothers: Claudio, who used to wrap me up and rub himself against my back when I was cold as a child, his calluses irritating my skin. Later he began to make me drink his slimy wretchedness, but then he'd take me tenderly by the hand and walk with me to school, telling me silly stories and protecting me with such attentiveness that the nights faded and it was to his arms that I ran when something troubled me. Ernesto, enclosed in the back room with my father organizing the business and convening hushed meetings, leaving the women out, protective and dismissive: *You shouldn't get involved in this, you don't know anything about it, this is a man's issue.* And we never found out anything. Ricardo, handsome and jovial, my mother doting on him, caressing his face and his hair as if entranced, as if she couldn't believe that so much beauty could actually be real, as if he'd been the extension and perfection of her very being. My friend, Cristina, dancing and laughing. She stopped laughing when we embraced each other anxiously. So much curiosity, so much passion at that age. I shouldn't have trembled that way when I pushed myself against her at that dance, I shouldn't have shuddered that way. She kept on dancing, rhythmically moving away from me. I watched her grow from the other side of the street, along with the young men from the neighborhood. None of them crossed the street to knock on my door but I didn't care. I only longed for Cristina. Pablo, to whom I first made love, without loving him, who told me with clenched teeth that I was frigid and dry, who didn't see my trembling from pain and revulsion. My Aunt Matilde, after whom I was baptized, combative and tough, with a propensity for taking to the streets, who chained herself to the iron fence outside Congress and was always appearing on the news and wouldn't speak to my father. Or to her son, because he disregarded the disappeared man who, in reality, wasn't his father but a carpetbagger who feigned to be paternal but humiliated and struck him, who stood always gazing from a faded, enlarged photograph, forever young while the rest of them grew older, a lustreless photograph that she would end up alone with in her coffin. Grandmother Esther, the worthless belonging of her husband, the two of them becoming musty in their coastal village with their lethargic and

104

tedious movements and *mate* in the center of the table. And the others, so many uncles, so many aunts, branches of cousins, swinging doors through which they enter and leave, but in the end, all minor celestial bodies in the constellation in which my mother is the sun and the black hole that swallows me, causes me to collapse into her light and into her night, that screams and suppresses, that silently contrives a way to strike even more harshly and brutally.

Ricardo, the handsome favorite son, acquired a film that showed a tempestuous sea breaking over rocks. Against the sound of the waves, the wind howled furiously. It was just a few minutes of film, but he taped the same scene over and over again so our mother would have a complete hour of sea to watch. Her body contorted toward the left, she drew close to the television and leaned on the screen, her hands turned teal blue by the flickering light, and then, smiling, and calm, she remained transfixed by the eternally restless swirling of that water.

She had to be bathed, fed, taken to the bathroom. When one could, when one was able to tolerate it. Standing in front of the screen, she let the urine run down her legs, didn't even bother to step aside from the pool that she'd left. We'd wash her with a sponge and put newspaper on the floor to prevent a disaster. We covered the mattress with plastic, and purchased a large clay pot and plastic containers, diapers, eau de cologne, sponges, more towels. In the beginning, we all helped take care of her. But soon, with time, the men became more and more disengaged. "You're a woman," they told me, "it's more appropriate for you." "She'd be embarrassed if we saw her naked." "She's your mother, you're her daughter." And soon they no longer even argued the issue, they simply slipped away, certain that I'd attend to her. To her and to the tumor that was deforming her.

I could no longer attend classes. I brought the certificates, did the paperwork, and remained imprisoned in the house, indolent in the eyes of others, confined among the wizened ones to whom I belonged.

"In time you'll be able to return to your courses," my father would say.

"They're not just courses, it's my career," I should have answered. I'd been thinking, "She can't last much longer." That's what we all thought. But she continued to survive. Mangled, languid, though still upright. Just like those massive, withered trees that cling with twisted roots to the clearing in the forest, surrounded by twisted, black branches.

We all got sick that winter. A flu epidemic. We fell ill, one after the other. She, on the other hand, no. She remained tethered to the smooth, disinterested sea, standing there barefoot, her hair braided with my forceful tugs, untangling the tresses with rage, every morning the comb ensnared in that snarled mass of seaweed.

"Don't cut her hair, absolutely not," my father would say. But he didn't have to wash it, so I took the scissors, escorted her to the bathroom and, in a matter of minutes, years of brilliant, golden locks fell to the floor. Without them, all the wrinkled angles, the flaccidity along the jawline, and the grayish skin of her lifeless face appeared. Her now short hair, also gray, stood perpendicular to her changed face. She then appeared to everyone like a house that's emerged in winter when the trees are bare, revealing the peeling paint and the damp wood.

The others stood looking at her and I climbed back into my bed and left them staring until they'd seen enough, until my father got up and, in those final days of winter, announced: "We're going to look for a place to take care of her." The others agreed and I heard him add, "You need to return to your classes. This is not a life." And he and his children turned around and I stood up. It was evident—it always was—that it couldn't go on any longer.

We took her in the car. "Someone has to take care of them," the woman insisted. "I take them in." She spoke with self-abnegation and affection, as if she really cared about the defenseless elderly, and yet the first thing she does is require all power over their pensions. She then emphatically charges the difference, and if a family doesn't pay, she takes the patient to the main consulting room and leaves her or him there. She calls the relatives and warns them that they can't return, that the space has been filled, even though there's always availability. The beds are moved closer together when necesary to accommodate another one.

If weather permits, they take chairs outside and the elderly sit on the sidewalk in a row close to the wall of the house to watch the street. The workers from the factory across the street wave and one of the elderly men smiles as if he thought he were the commander of the crew that was finishing its shift. Another mutters, "They're just a bunch of lowlifes. This neighborhood keeps getting worse." The elderly boarders die one after another and are replaced by another just like them.

In the rooms to the rear of the house are the bedridden. The bedroom accommodates four or five beds, allowing a narrow aisle which the hired help drift through twice daily giving them their pablum and changing their diapers.

In the front of the house are the other bedrooms, with windows that open up to the street. That's where they placed my mother, with her television in front of her and the endless video of the sea. "You're going to have to pay us for the added expense to the electric bill," the owner of the facility informs us. When the video ends, she screams, a loud and exasperated shriek. While they calm her down, she lowers her tone of voice and complains pitifully. One of her hands flaps impatiently until the furious sea returns to strike at the screen.

Chairs, chairs and more chairs. They're moved from one place to another. Around the dining room table and living room, chairs against the wall facing the open window that looks out onto the tiled patio which is crossed by clotheslines and holds trash containers. Chairs moved when the sun comes out. The elderly residents slumped in their chairs, their eyes closed, breathing the warm air. Chairs taken outside, chairs brought back inside. I lean against the wall for support. Once and for all, let this dragging of chairs outside and inside cease.

I take the bus every day to see her. The others appear when they're able. Occasionally, a Sunday at noon, they give her cookies or chocolates, speak sweetly to her and then are back on the streets. She turns to them, smiles for an instant, and goes back to the screen. She nibbles the sweets, drools, and I clean her.

My mother always used French perfume and various creams. She'd place one foot on the bathtub and scrub her entire body, caressing herself from head to foot, her eyes half open, while she watched her skin glow.

"If you're going to stand there staring at me like some imbecile, at least scrub my back," she'd say. She'd extend herself on the bed and I'd massage her languid body and breathe in the aroma of soap and lavender.

My father says that everything spent on her has been a waste. His new woman uses creams. What we take to my mother are cheap ointments that smell oily,

"Don't go this afternoon," Rocio tells me.

She's a friend from the institute. Actually, my only friend. I'm not her favorite. She's surrounded by people who find her enthusiasm and energy contagious. At times she radiates toward me and drags me somewhere. With her, I've come to know the hidden bars of the grand avenues and those renovated dance salons in private homes that open in the early hours of the morning. She likes large, diverse gatherings, mingling and connecting. It's difficult to tell her no.

"Tell me, what's going to change today if you don't go?"

She looks me in the eye and tells me that I go from my classes to hospice, and then to my home, where I'm enslaved.

"It's not hospice. It's a retirement home," I reply mindlessly.

In reality, I don't have a response that convinces her. She takes me by the arm and we head to the center of town. We have to stand while riding the bus and, leaning against my arm, she tells me, "I just discovered it. It's like any other house, but inside everything is happening. You can't let me down. Matilde, you can't. This time, no way."

She then begins an enthusiastic discourse about immobility.

"If you don't move and go to other places, nothing happens. It's as simple as this: Seated in your house, looking out the window, everything will remain the same. Everything happens out there, just steps away. You take a couple steps forward and you're in a world where everything is possible, everything. Seize your radiant youth, as afterward, nothing happens, nothing."

The inflection in her voice changes, her almond-shaped face is illuminated, and we head to the metro. With her, time truly flies. We walk along the tree-lined streets, in a darkness that parts like black spiderwebs. She finds the doors, makes gestures, and continues inside. There's always something better beyond, more distant.

It's an older house with a dance floor in the main patio outside. Rocio speaks to the young men, looking them squarely in the eyes. She's attractive, although not sufficiently to rely on her good looks, so she compensates with a brazen flirt. We seat ourselves at a plastic table, on plastic chairs, and we ask for a Pisco with Coca-Cola. I'm not fond of alcohol, but Rocio dismisses my objection.

"How can you survive the night without it?" she asks while she licks the edge of the glass and looks at me with semi-shut eyes. The angle of her glance is directed at me, but it transcends me and goes further, toward those seated nearby. She's acting for a broad, imaginary audience, which she continues to do while she drags me to the dance floor and dances, fixated on her body, which gyrates, stretching and swaying and swelling with desire, in a cadence that's sinuous and vertical, beginning and ending merely so that others can watch. I accompany her, eyes wide open, my body tense, muscles tight, invisible in the center of a dance floor from which I'll exit alone. Rocio, content, dancing from one guy to the other, making gestures to me with no regard for my decision. Disappearing into the distance, I slip away, raising a rukus after paying the bill.

Ricardo often danced with my mother. They'd embrace and spin across the terrace. My father swelled with pride and extended his hand, but she pretended not to see it. He'd then take me by the waist and we'd whirl unrhythmically around the terrace. I'd trip on the uneven flagstones and we'd be forced to sit down and watch. I'd let out a forced laugh to forget my ineptitude and he'd drink more wine. He never missed having a drink as he gazed at her and saw the tiny waist of his wife.

The video of the sea focuses on the breakwater, the foam formed as it crashes against the rocks near the beach. The massive, green waves wail, rising up against the rocks until the sun pierces through them and transforms the mass of water into a smooth, thin wave that retreats. It's a fragile crystal that's broken over and over. She watches, totally absorbed, and her hunched body sways to the rhythm of a breeze no one else feels. She doesn't respond, doesn't look at me, she evades me if I touch her. But there's a moment when the camera focuses on the cliffs, the plateau of yellow meadows, and the precipice. She then remains still, very still and expectant, and she looks at me with her pupils dilated and her mouth half-open. She can no longer see the sea. It's barely heard in the background. She takes my hand and squeezes it forcefully, enraged. She tilts her head and it appears that she's going to speak, that she's going to say something sweet and tender. She's no longer the invalid, sick old woman. But the beautiful woman she once was never returns. She ceases to be herself, and I find myself in her eyes and become her, with a young girl clinging to my skirt, tugging at it, feigning complacent smiles and caressing the curve of her hips, the smooth fabric tight against her body. As soon as the waves appear, she detaches herself, brusquely turning away to face the image on the screen and I'm no longer there. But for some seconds, I was there, and she was submissive to me and I felt that she was complacent.

A few older gentlemen arrive. "I'll just be here for a while," they insist, somewhat ashamed. They resist, become desperate. In a matter of days, they're huddled over.

They keep adding beds and there's no longer space among them. Who cares. They're either sprawled out on their beds or dumbfounded in their wheelchairs, looking at the patio and at those underneath the eaves, in the shadows of clothing hanging from the clothesline, so much clothing hung from those lines.

There's a dog that wanders and stops near the first person who talks to her. I've never seen her leave, and yet she gets pregnant and ends up giving birth to six puppies. The elderly pass the puppies among themselves, from lap to lap. They squeeze them with desperation. The pups' mother watches them desperately without harming or attacking them, simply observing her offspring being passed through the air, cradled in shawls, and stretched out against the emaciated and withered bodies that nobody touches, grasping for something warm and beating, in a feigned and brusque gesture.

My grandmother, Matilde, once had a black, ferocious dog. It had been her husband's, who'd disappeared. When he didn't return, the dog stopped barking, running, digging in the yard and destroying the shrubs. She'd take him with her when she went out to march along the streets with those bearing photos of young men across their chests. They walked together, without any leash or gestures. Grandmother once mentioned to my father that a dog would keep her company in the absence of her son. That her son preferred to side with the kidnappers and assassins so he could make money, selling them trinkets. My father would respond, "What is it that you haven't understood? He wasn't my father. He never could or would be. Bury that miserable man once and for all."

My mother didn't allow pets. The lizards, rabbits, cats, and dogs my brothers brought home disappeared, as did the dove that I'd cared for over a weekend. I returned home from school and it was no longer there. "It flew away," she told me. But it had a broken wing, which I'd bandaged, and that cat was there rummaging through the trash.

Not all of the residents are elderly. Some are middle-aged and are either invalids or have some other disability. There's even a younger woman, beautiful and composed.

"A deep depression," she says smiling, with an odd air of pride. Her eyes wander from side to side, while her body leans against the wall.

She refuses to touch dogs, yet she approaches the elderly, takes their hands and caresses them with tenderness while they speak and she listens, head tilted, gazing around her. Or she sings to them rhythmically and, at times, even dances, humming, grasping their arms, inviting them to follow her from their wheelchairs.

"With them I feel content. Everything out there's so foreign."

I know that she's not speaking to me but to herself. The sea that my mother sought to possess no longer matters, nor that I haven't moved to take care of her. She keeps looking at me and speaking.

I'm all too familiar with the cycle of the film. Every time the episode that moves her appears, I return to accompany her. The rest of the time I look over her things to make certain that everything's in order, that they provide her with personal supplies and change her sheets. I give her cookies or candy, I speak with the woman in charge so she's aware that I'm always vigilant. Or I try to read and catch up with my classes.

My father waits for three months to introduce to us the woman who will be replacing our mother. A woman with small children moves into our home and she begins to chase me out.

Her children take over all the rooms in the house. They bring their furniture and tear down the walls. "Just some partitions," she insists. The rooms are left spacious but without private spaces in which to hide. I'm reduced to moving into the bedroom of her youngest daughter. Rosy walls, curtains and a bedspread with images of children's movies, toys spread out all over the floor.

"Do you want to take tea with me?" she asks, seated at her wooden table, the four chairs occupied by her dolls. She's a chubby, boorish child. What should have been smooth, lustrous skin has been transformed into something rough. It's still day when she turns out the lights and goes to sleep.

I go to the dining room and make an improvised bed, a corner where I can escape with my books and my schoolwork. My father's woman tells me again and again that I should leave, get a life. She insists to him in a melodic voice that I'm of the age to leave home as my brothers did, and that I should find a place of my own.

My father doesn't respond. He prohibited me from going out at night or walking alone, but now remains silent. He doesn't even lower his shameful glance. He nods in approval and looks at me differently, as if she'd revealed something repulsive.

"I'm not even twenty," I blurt out.

"At your age, I already had my oldest son and had my life mapped out," he responds.

"Now all that's been undone, right? That perfect life has evaporated," I should tell him. Or scream at him, "Grandmother was right. She preferred a dead man over you."

But she's been buried for years and he's never brought flowers to her grave. So I remain silent, retreating to my corner, occupying myself with my few belongings, hoping that my presence will bother them, that my silence screams to her that he continues to keep his wife alive and sickly and I'm still here to remind her of that.

"Cookies, did you bring me cookies?"

They remain seated in their wheelchairs, looking at my hands, my backpack, as I always bring them something. They turn toward me, anxious, perhaps hopeful for something that will break their monotonous daily routine. Soon they become disenchanted and turn away. Or maybe they just don't have the strength to tolerate the effort.

I wait until the video ends, then turn off the device at that exact moment. I take her by the hand and lead her to the patio and fresh air. Although she walks hunched over, she can still walk. The doctor has assured me that the tumor hasn't yet taken over.

I whisper in her ear, telling her who's there so she'll greet them. She observes them with her head tilted and smiles at them. It's a twisted smile, but her eyes become brilliant and coquettish.

"Here is don Alejo," and we approach a middle-aged gentleman who lost his legs while working in the mines. He's cautious, reserved. He clips fragments of sacred texts, and if someone is careless, he forcefully takes them by the hand and reads aloud to them, without a breath, impossible to interrupt.

"This is the word of God," he says looking to the heavens.

Today he has his hair slicked back and is wearing a suitcoat. The caregiver hands out corn whiskey in plastic glasses. They're celebrating because he asked her to marry him. He's finally going to have someone to take care of him "Just me," he says tearfully. "God provides, and He takes away. My family abandoned me when they believed me to be useless and now God is giving me a new home."

He's the only one who doesn't drink. The others empty their glasses within seconds, thirsty and enthused, clicking their tongues against their bare gums, licking their dry and lifeless lips.

My mother's lips were very voluptuous. She applied an intense red lipstick and then a gloss. Her hair surrounded her face and in the center, that glossy red fruit somewhat open, like a pomegranate. My father would grab her from behind, bury his head in that tangled mess of blonde mane and breathe in deeply. He then turned her toward him and kissed her, hugging her tightly, devouring her with kisses and drooling over her, and yet her lips never lost their crimson color.

One gentleman is strapped in his wheelchair. He constantly twists and turns, trying to stand up, and struggles with the strap that keeps him in eternally vertical, bent at a right angle.

"I want to go to the bathroom," he whimpers. "I need to go to the bathroom."

The caretakers walk past him. I tell them don Carlos needs to stand up and they respond by insisting that he always complains about the same thing.

"There now, just keep quiet," they tell him in childlike tones. I hope he has an accident in his pants, but he lives with it for hours. He keeps enduring and perhaps the caretakers were right and he's just trying to get attention.

The younger woman is no longer there. The caretakers tell me she threw herself onto the rails of the metro. She said she was going shopping at the store on the corner, but instead walked to the metro station and, without a second thought, threw herelf under the train.

"Don't say anything to her grandparents," they warn me.

An elderly woman says, "These aren't my hands."

If she sees her reflection in the window, she whimpers, "This isn't my face."

She then addresses someone nearby. "Honestly, something's happening to me, they're transforming me. This isn't me. What are they doing to me here? What exactly are they doing? Please!"

Another elderly woman approaches, observes her face in the mirror, then cries silently and doesn't say another word.

My mother never cried. "Don't tell me your misfortunate misery," she'd say. She still doesn't cry. She merely whimpers when she needs to see the sea. She doesn't have wrinkles like the other elderly patients do, formed by tears on the cheeks of the others. Her skin is still taunt, unwrinkled.

They all have beds, bedspreads worn or deteriorated. The children of one of the invalids purchased a beautiful hospital bed for her. The toothless mouths of the elderly expose their anxiousness, their needs. Their meager desires are totally physical. All most of them have left is flesh about to rot and they cling to their deteriorating skin.

On the other hand, the invalid seems transparent between the white sheets on her bed, which elevates and inclines. She opens her mouth to scream, a soft yet profound sound, an elegant cry in ceaseless pain. Even with the morphine, I hear the underlying pain of broken bones.

"She's been here a year. The doctor insisted that she wouldn't be able to hold on much longer."

Agony and death. There's nothing else to await. We wait, expecting the tumor that's been silently waiting to strike. My mother sees the woman because her bed's close to the television. When the thunderous breaking of the waves happens, she stretches her hand to the bed. Still watching the screen, she rocks back and forth and says compassionately, "There, there, it's all right, all right." Her intent is not to calm her, but rather to silence her during the stellar moment of the waves crashing on shore.

My mother only rocked my brother. She'd embrace Ricardo and nestle him in her lap. "Everything's fine, my handsome child." She comforted him to the point of scratching him. She looked at me with disgust when I showed her the burns on my arm.

She refused to listen; she was older and didn't care. Nor did she ask me anything. If she had, perhaps I'd have told her other things. She didn't ask and I wasn't able to tell her how they did it, how much it hurt, what skin smells like

114

after it's been burned, how the fire was reflected in the outraged eyes of others.

"You're obsessed with those decrepit old people. Who cares about them?"

"Nobody, not even their relatives. Much less our family," Rocio adds.

There are five of us in our group. One of them says it's better not to face old age and death.

"In the end we'll all be confronted by it, so why worry and anticipate it."

Another adds that the elderly are just bothersome. One of the woman tightens up and shudders when she says they're disgusting. All agree that it's not the responsibility of any of us. I'm not sure why I'm watching the clock as they speak. Two minutes and seventeen seconds are spent on the topic. We then continue with the particulars.

"Live your life." With those words, the dialogue ends.

Rocio adds, "If you're going to work in communications, you can't be so annoying. This is sound advice and you should be thanking me."

She's exasperated with me. I, too, am tired of many things, yet say nothing.

When we've finished, we go out dancing. This time I have a drink. It's hot and Rocio perspires in the center of the dance floor. Her skin is brilliant and the dampness of her perspiring arms glistens a bluish tint to the beat of the intermittent lights. Her entire body is like a serpent that writhes and twists. The warm venom that emanates from her is sizzling and sweet like an essential oil of sandalwood and violet.

I kiss her. I force her mouth open and thrust my tongue, licking the excessive sweat on her face, clinging to her damp body and soaking mine, an aroused emission that melds incense and oil.

"Disgusting," she tells me. Even though she's pushing me away, I continue to cling to her and she speaks, her mouth on mine.

"Disgusting, repulsive," she repeats. Her saliva falls on my lips, the breath of every word rises to my palate, and my fingers touch her quivering throat when she says, "Disgusting! You smell like the elderly!"

She pushes me and it seems like her hands sink into my skin. She moves away, yet the traces of her still linger, warm and exhausted, on my clothing and skin. She walks away with her head lifted, stiffly, sternly, her back straight, despising me, a resilient vertical post that within a few steps gives way to three dance steps and is lost among the crowd without turning around or looking at me.

I run down the street. The buses pass by me. I don't want to ride them or even stop running. I tire and walk a while then continue to run, not allowing myself to feel the warm breeze this December night. The buses keep passing by.

I arrive at the home of the elderly and enter through an open window. Nobody would steal their stenchy rags, their Christmas decorations with burned-out lights, their medicine, or their misery.

I climb into her bed and cling to her side. Her nightgown is rolled up to her chest and she's naked below. She complains, protests, uttering intelligible words. It's been a while since she's been coherent. I hug her and whisper into her ear the sound of the sea, of the water washing over the damp sand. Gently I reproduce the furious roar of the waves striking the rocks and rising up against the salty breeze.

She avoids me and I feel her warm urine running down my naked leg. The liquid soon becomes cold, burning my skin before it dries, before it evaporates metallically, glacially, leaving me there, embracing a body that's withering away, a body which was once voluptuous and restless, which never resembled yet now mirrors mine, just like those that stalk me.

Japanese Garden

Children lie, every one of them. Some do it because it's in their best interests. Others because they're afraid. Some lie because they're cunning and ambitious, deceitfully slandering others for their own personal gain. There are children who lie to be loved, as if it were impossible for them to be shown affection as they are. All of them lie. And all of them are discovered in their lies. They blush, retract, sure of themselves. For whatever reason they end up betrayed and their chins tremble. They try to deny it. Or they hide and cry alone. But they're already trapped.

I don't lie. I watch them. I see their crafty ways, the vigilant gazes of adults and the traps they set to surprise them. I watch obsessively, making mental notes. I register everything. Then I rehearse in front of a mirror and observe my gestures, every detail of my unemotional face, the shaking of my hands, my body language tense and controlled. Conviction, above all, conviction. When

I'm ready, absolutely prepared, I begin to speak. And I try to say a few words that are true. Very few. None, I hope.

"Your mother never stopped talking," my grandmother tells me. "And she liked to hum, play the guitar and impress others. She was loud and theatrical and needed to be the center of attention, with everyone watching and praising her." She says it despairingly, so I remain silent so I don't seem like her. At times, I ask her if my mother did this or that and then I do the opposite. I'm more and more distinct. Grandmother smiles and hugs me and her entire body trembles with joy.

Grandfather watches television. He's addicted to the news. He has the television placed diagonally, so that he can see it from both the sofa and the dining room. On top of the television, Grandmother placed a crocheted doily and a vase of plastic flowers. She insists that having a television in the center of the home is a vulgarity. Regardless, she sits in front of the television to watch soap operas and turns up the volume for the morning programming while she does her daily chores.

The deliveryman from the corner store brings bread and milk. If he's bringing several things, he grabs the bicycle and loads them into the basket. Sometimes he takes me for a ride, and we turn around at the corner. I steady myself on the metallic frame looking ahead, my arms firmly grasping his sides. He parks in front of the back door of the store and goes to the bathroom. I hear him flush the toilet. He emerges combing his hair.

"Marines sail all over the world and meet women. I'd like to be a Marine and force myself on all of them," he says. He runs his tongue over his lips enticingly and his gaze is watery. I climb off and he takes off pedaling. Grandmother says he's an imbecile without direction.

Grandfather talks to the television. Rather, he screams at it furiously. "What are you going to say now, you corrupt and loud-mouthed old man. Shut up, stupid shits. You only talk to women who discuss fashion or cuisine."

The insults to the men, in some way, are respectful. He confers upon them a certain prestige: thieves, schemers, damned. In case of the women he mutters, "Bitches, whores, go back to your kitchens."

In the garden in front there's a tree with leaves that resemble stars. It's an old tree, very large and overgrown. When spring arrives, it turns green again.

You'd think there'd be no more room for so much growth. The leaves curl around the fragile branches and form a thick, damp mat. It's a Japanese maple, Grandmother tells me; a very exotic and special tree. Not everyone has one. She's proud of it, and around the base she plants petunias very year, as if the flowers paid respect to its height. She told me my mother was never interested in plants, so I kneel on the ground and pull the weeds, I stomp around the tree and place small white stones. One day I convince Grandmother to buy a small, brightly colored elf to place in the garden. It looks precious next to the tree, but Grandfather says it's a monstrosity and with a kick destroys it. "I could have drowned it, ignorant child."

I cry but he insists that nobody places stupid elves in his home.

The entrance hall is filled with framed photos along the wall. In almost every photograph my grandfather is wearing a uniform. Grandmother appears so young, always with a gold-plated brooch: the image is that of a flower with a hummingbird hovering and sipping its nectar. "When you marry, I'll give it to you," she tells me. It's a gaudy piece of jewelry, but since my mother didn't like it, I tell my grandmother that it's the one thing I most hope to have. My grandmother's hairdo is like a million question marks upon her head. My grandfather is two heads taller than she is. There are no photos of my mother on this wall or on any other wall. Their dog's name is Milu.

"She's an old, stinky dog," my grandfather declares. "One of these days I'm going to shoot her." And he kicks her if she comes too close to the couch. When she was a puppy, she belonged to my mother. When she went away, she didn't take the dog with her.

The dog has grown up frightened, with her tail between her hind legs. I'm also not fond of her as she's always afraid and looks to the heavens with her canine eyes. They promised me that when the dog dies, I can have a cat, a cleaner animal. "If we're lucky, it will get lost among the tiles on the roof," my grandfather adds, roaring with laughter.

Every time I lose a tooth, the mouse brings me a coin. No blood comes from my gums: my teeth fall out slowly and silently. They leave a space of soft, open contours with a metallic taste. My grandfather insists that I won't bleed because I'm losing them much later than normal so their roots are dry. The teeth fall like autumn leaves, small and holey they slide over my tongue.

The neighbors to the right are evangelicals and don't drink alcohol.

"That's wonderful," my grandmother says.

"I bet they imbibe in secret and do dirty things," my grandfather replies. "Besides, they're effeminate, repressed gays, which is worse than loose women."

The neighbors to the left grill outside every weekend. The aroma of meat on the grill wafts throughout the neighborhood, and then my grandfather finds any justification to visit them and stay for a long time. From our patio, we hear his powerful, guttural voice. "Do you know what we should do with them? Kill them all!" If he had his way, over half the population would be dead.

In the bedroom that once belonged to my mother, they set up a sewing room. And in the tiny room where the sewing machine once stood, they set up my bed. My grandmother is often asked to sew dresses and skirts, but mainly she is asked to alter clothing they already have. The women bring bags of ragged clothing and Grandmother asks us to please be quiet while her clients are there. I'm aware that she's warning not me but my grandfather. He mutters that if it weren't for his miserable pension, he wouldn't allow, even for a minute, those damn women in his house.

Grandfather insists that ignorance is dangerous. And not knowing the history of our country is even worse. According to him, that's harmful for both the mind and the soul. I memorize the names of all the cities in Chile from north...Arica, Iquique, Topopilla, Chañaral, Copiapo. Caldera, Vallenar...to south...Punta Arenas and Puerto Williams and there's not one single place that he that he doesn't know. He explains to me that the homeland enters through the eyes, then the mind and, from there, the heart, where it forever stays. And it enters through the ears with Chilean music, through the mouth with every bite of the food of each region, and through the skin in each climate zone. "It also enters in other ways that I can't tell you," and he bursts out in a hearty laugh.

Every once in awhile my mother attempts to communicate with us. Someone approaches Grandmother in the street, in the store, wherever, and hands her a piece of paper with the date, time and place where she's going to wait for us—what they call, in combat, the coordinates.

Grandfather is at home, but Grandmother never tells him we're going to meet her. "If he knew, he might arrive ranting," she explains. Sometimes it's a park, other times a supermarket. There have been special places, like the hospital or the cemetery. There are always a lot of people and we don't recognize her until she approaches and speaks to us. She wears wigs and strange clothing, transforming herself from a young woman to an elderly woman, from elegant to vulgar. She moves us aside and when she's certain nobody can see us, she hugs me tenaciously. She asks me to tell her about myself, but I don't know what to say. How should I know what would make her proud when we barely know each other and, at times, so many months and seasons have passed. When she repeats over and over again: "Manuela, Manuela, my precious Manuela," Grandmother turns away with a look of disgust.

Grandfather insists that naming me Manuela was a stupid decision by my mother. "Just one more among so many bad ideas." He adds that they're going to make fun of me because men know that the name Manuela refers to a blow job, masturbating, and other expressions I don't understand. But clearly, it's indecorous and insulting.

At school there are other girls with the same name as mine and no one laughs at their name. Or mine.

"Wait until you grow up. You'll find out, stubborn child," Grandfather says.

There's a cabinet with glass doors. Grandmother tells me to never open those doors. "Never touch anything inside that cabinet," she insists as she shuts the fragile, leaded glass doors after removing the teapots and hand painted teacups. She never removes the lacey fans or the decorative pieces. She serves tea to her friends on a round table draped with an embroidered tablecloth. The aroma of warm tea and toasted bread inundates the room. Whispers of women and the clinking of fine china. Outside the dogs bark and at the corner, buses roar past. From the second floor of the house I can hear sacred music from next door and the televisions blasting at full volume from the other neighbors. Grandfather snores, the springs in his bed groaning.

No one steals anything from Grandmother. She knows what's in each place and the precise moment when something is moved. I never rummage through her things or remove anything, not even hiding a coin of hers in my pocket.

We barely hear about my father. Grandfather says he was an imbecile and that I needn't know anything else. That at this point, he must be incarcerated or dead, that I should be grateful for never knowing him. Grandmother insists that he was an idealist; perhaps wayward, but, nonetheless an idealist.

"What's an idealist?"

"A dreamer with impossible goals," Grandmother responds.

"Your mother became infatuated with him, that's all. We spent so much money educating her and she took off with the first delinquent that crossed her path." That's how my Grandfather speaks. I have difficulty understanding him because he responds only once and never repeats what he said. "If she'd wanted someone who'd take her for a fool, she could have made a better choice," he adds.

There once was a garden in the back. I never saw it, but Grandmother told me that she grew vegetables and herbs until her mother-in-law became ill and Grandfather built a room over her garden.

"With my own hands, for my dear mother," he states with pride. He visits her twice a day and sits beside her to read. He continues his litany of declarations of love for her and his self-complacency. The elderly woman doesn't move, or even blink. Strokes have left her bedridden. Grandmother spoon feeds her, changes her diapers and bathes her. Every couple of weeks, a nurse's aide comes to look in on her. They place her on a chair, wrapped in a shawl, and leave her in the front patio. Hunched over, she obliviously takes in the sun. Her breathing is loud.

"Still, she doesn't die," my Grandmother mutters.

The children of the Front came from the north to stay with their grandmother. First they'd incarcerated their father and then his wife. Their elderly grandmother was overwhelmed by the new expenses and began to sell little pieces of paper. "Suspicious little scraps of paper," Grandfather asserts. They all help her to weigh, pack, and label the packages. On occasion the youngest child, with her braids and a gaudy dress, accompanies them to make deliveries. Her older brother follows closely behind, pretending to follow her. On her way home, she buys ice cream and returns content, having carried out her task with perfection. On Sundays they all go to visit their parents. They take them bundles of food and who knows what else and return later in the evening. If the curtains aren't drawn, I can see the boys cleaning a pistol and wrapping knives in a cloth. "They're all delinquents," my Grandfather alleges. "And this can only go from bad to worse: traffickers everywhere. They're forming gangs. This is just the beginning."

I'm intrigued by that word, *trafficker*. "The word *criminal* is also attractive," he tells me, "but you never want to encounter one of them." He raises my skirt and squeezes my buttocks with one hand while the other closes tight around my neck. "This is the least they'd do to you, stupid girl."

He owns three guns. "Don't touch them," he cautions. "Never aim, at anyone, but if you have to, never doubt!" One day he'll teach me, but not yet, not until I have "firm hands instead of those flaccid worms that you call fingers."

Sometimes some of Grandfather's old companions stop by. They sit in the dining room and over lunch they recall anecdotes, boasting about their feats and refilling their glasses as they sing military marches at the top of their lungs. By dusk they're singing songs in German, war tunes and "La Marseillaise." When they have imbibed too much and have let their guards down, they embrace each other and chant:

> I had a comrade
> Another like him you'll never find
> Always marching alongside me
> And if the bugle called us to arms
> He was there stepping up and keeping pace.

They pound the table and Grandmother's decorations all shake. Every once in a while they stand up and, teetering, sing the national anthem. Their voices rise when they sing the part "your renowned, valiant soldiers." They'd all hoped to be heroes in some war, to have battle wounds and bloody memories. Maybe that explains why their eyes fill with tears when they sing: "...and the stars testify to the honorous wounds of war..." I can't sneak a peek to watch them, because if I do, they'll oblige me to march in single file with them, teach me to stand erectly, and to give the war salute, requesting my survival backpack to inspect it.

There's an enormous jail just a few blocks from our house. The solid, expansive walls have barbed wire on top and there are towers with armed guards to keep watch. On Sundays there's visitation and the families form a line to enter. The prisoners hang their washed clothing in the windows, so the walls seem strangely colorful. Grandmother tells me that everyone knows when someone enters but not when or how they leave. Given that the prison is a school for criminals, people inside learn to be even more evil. I'd like to enter the jail to see the rooms, the patios, and the place where they wash their clothing.

"If they condemned people for asking stupid questions, you'd already be there," Grandfather assures me.

I attach the buttons. I sew them with doubled thread and make a cross, passing through the fabric and then the holes in a diagonal pattern. I finish off on the back side of the garment, leaving the ends of the thread just above the surface, which gives the impression that the sewing will soon undo itself. Grandmother turns on the radio and we listen to boleros and tangos. Further off is the television and the alarming news. Barricades and protests. Just a few blocks away. Our door is closed, our gates are imposingly tall.

"Stop sewing and come and learn something useful," Grandfather tells me. "Ignorance is deplorable," he insists over and over again. So he teaches me to recite the list of presidents from the past to the present: Manuel Blanco Encalada, Ramon Freire, Francisco Pinto, Francisco Ramon Vicuña, Jose Tomas Ovalle, and when we get to modern times, I say Alessandri, Frei very softly and rapidly add Allende, because even though he was useless, he still existed, and then, energetically and with fervor, I scream Pinochet, the savior of our country! And Grandfather adds the following: "Since 1973, our glorious President who eradicated Communism and saved us from a civil war. Contemporary hero. We have living proof of history. No one can come to us with other tales."

In the summer we travel to the naval base in Talcahuano, where my uncle's destined to be stationed. He's an engineer and works in a shipyard, where they fix the hulls of ships. My cousins are small and at times they entrust me with them. I take them for walks on the seaside promenade in their strollers and on tricycles. They take off noisily, sure of themselves, as if land and sea belong to them.

Aunt Margot is totally disorganized. In a dresser drawer I discover some porcelain figurines. She surely doesn't remember that she has them, so I don't consider it a sin if I take a gray cat with a reddish tongue playing with a skein of crimson wool.

In the port are yachts and sailboats. Beyond that, the factory that produces fish flour. Depending on the direction of the wind, the smell drifts toward the houses. Pestilent waves wash over the seawall. Grandfather spends the days with his son. He puts on his best suit, slicks back his hair, and shaves every day. Grandmother dedicates herself to cooking, cleaning and helping with household chores. In the afternoon, I grab the children and their strollers, not because I want to be with them, but because I need to get out and distance myself from all of them.

Here also they sing war songs. My aunt is a French teacher, and even though she's never worked, she still pronounces the words to "La Marseillaise" carefully. Uncle Jose explains to us that it's the most beautiful song in the world and that when Napoleon heard it, he declared that such a song would save him many cannons. We march to the rhythm, brooms and dusters like weapons over our shoulders. Knees high, back straight, and a military salute.

Q'un sang impur abreuve nos sillons translates to "an impure blood drenches our furrows." They want to kill them all, just like Grandfather. Until the enemy's blood runs through the ploughed and sown fields and turns them, I think, crimson red.

I've never seen my blood, not even a drop from my nose, knees, teeth, nowhere. My skin wraps around this blood of mine, and it's never had contact with air. Never has a breath of air entered my bloodstream.

"In mechanics, they refer to this as packaging," Grandfather tells me. "A solid packaging ensures that no water enters the motor and mixes with the oil."

My cousins are always bleeding. They fall and begin to bleed. They pick at their scabs and bleed again. They run and streams of thick blood escape from their noses. They wash it off and continue running so that the chilly wind stops the bleeding and turns the blood solid and black.

At the top of the hill is the country club. They give me a pass so I can enter. "Take the children with you," insists Aunt Margot. I place one of them on the swings and I allow the other to go up and down the slide. The youngest stays in the stroller observing his hands. I run among the trees, singing the songs that I like and invent choreographic moves to dance there among the thickets, just like my mother. Because no one sees me, it's as if I don't exist.

Uncle Jorge takes us sailing in the sailboat. All of us wear orange life jackets. Fierce wind bites our faces and our frozen hands grasp the ropes during abrupt movements. Grandfather's wearing a sailor's cap, clinging to the helm with eyes half-closed, his face frozen stiff, and his chest inflated. The keel splits the waves and the small vessel rises and falls. The sea is so vast and deep, and it seems like the farther we move from the coast, the water is even more dense, immense and unending.

The middle child was born with Down's Syndrome, and it's difficult for him to close his mouth, so my aunt keeps a cloth mask over his face. When he speaks, the words sound strange, as if he had a hot potato in his mouth. Grandfather acts as if he didn't exist, not even addressing him by his name. "Martin, Martin, Martin," I say while tickling his belly. He laughs and drools even more. When they put on his pajamas, he touches his lower parts, stretches and contorts his erect, fleshy penis, laughs, and drools a bit more.

Martin is blonde with blue eyes. There's no one in the family who's so fair in complexion, with such transparent skin. Grandmother looks sternly at Aunt Margot and tells her that it's very strange. Grandfather alleges that the nurses are always chattering and place the infants wherever. It's not surprising that they fouled up and mistakenly switched him in the hospital. My aunt insists that she saw him when he was born and is certain that this is her son, a special and different child.

"In our family there's never been anyone sickly or strange."

"He's a little angel, a gift from God."

The kitchen smells like the sea. Like fish and seaweed, stagnant water and salt. My aunt is always daydreaming and dries her hands obsessively on her apron. She never speaks to the children and they play quietly. When my Uncle Jorge arrives, she arranges her hair and takes cocktails to the gentlemen. Grandmother accompanies her with a tray of appetizers. The women don't drink, but are attentive to the men's desires and serve them constantly. Grandfather complains: "Why did you add capers to the fish?" "What happened that you didn't make toast?" "This drink tastes like syrup. Don't you know how to prepare a decent drink?" He looks at his son and smiles with satisfaction at his powerful display of dominance.

I remember one day when my mother hugged me and said it was a shame that I was born female. "Countless hardships await you," she murmured in my ear.

"Women are indecent," Grandfather states emphatically. "Though homosexuals are even worse," he adds.

I walk to school. The vigilant nun at the entrance of the school examines each student from head to toe and removes earrings and bracelets and ties back their hair if they're wearing it loosely. "She's the gatekeeper," the adults say. I arrive impeccable, never has anyone said anything to me; plus they smile at me.

Grandfather adores his country. "It's my love, my life and I'd give my blood for it." He tells me about the great battles, the ones in Rancagua, Chacabuco, Maipu, El Roble, Yerbas Buenas, the naval combat at Iquique. He's overcome with emotion by the lives of the great heroes, Pedro de Valdivia, O'Higgins, Carrera, Arturo Prat. But we must never forget the latest war, the great war against Communism that was won by Pinochet and his three commanders: Leigh, Merino, and Mendoza.

The Mapuche don't count as heroes; they were enemies from the very beginning.

"Don't get any ideas in your head. Lautaro, Galvarino, Caupolican are all Indians, just Indians. Even worse, they were indomitable. And drunkards. And heretics. They didn't have one ounce of heroism in their nasty, naked and ignorant bodies."

Consequently, in the history classes I know more than the others. When I speak, I feel the blood lost by our heroic soldiers and I can hear their valiant cries of war.

From the classrooms on the third floor, we can see the walls with barbed wire surrounding the jail. It houses only men, who spend the day locked away without anything to do. The nuns tell us that we have to pray for them, so that they repent and thus God will forgive them.

The girls are careless, leaving their backpacks scattered, exposed. It's very easy to select amid such disorder, to hide items until it's safe to take them.

From time to time, letters from my mother arrive. She reveals nothing about herself for fear they may be intercepted, but simply gives me advice. What I should do, what I should think, what I should never have to do, and the significance of everything. In each paragraph she notes: "Right now you won't understand me, but in the future I know you will. Keep these letters and at a later time, reread them, always read them, because in them I'm talking to you now and I'll continue to speak to you tomorrow." Grandmother tells me that if Grandfather were to see the letters, he'd be infuriated, so she orders me to look at them for a long time and then she burns them in an ashtray or she tears them up before tossing them in the garbage.

Raquel has curly red hair. She speaks with a soothing, high-pitched voice. At times I imitate that way of half-closing one's eyes, passing the tongue delicately around the mouth and then talking. Grandmother tells me that she's pretentious, but even so, she's my friend.

Sometimes I read for my great-grandmother. It's a recipe book. Ingredients, preparation, cooking directions. It features mixtures and blends that are reserved before moving on to something else. I like the sound of that word: *reserved*. They prepare other ingredients then return to what had been reserved and at that moment, the entire dish makes sense. She doesn't move, nor does she say anything.

"Where's she coming from, claiming this is her favorite book," Grandfather says. "If I tell you that this is the one she likes, it's because it's the one she likes," he states. "And I don't want you to be reading trash to my mother."

It's a pity that Grandfather's work in the auto shop is often only half a day. But at least it gets him out of the house for awhile and helps pay the bills. This is what Grandmother tells her best friend, Señora Ema. She's what's called a confidant.

I have a backpack ready in case of an emergency. Inside there's a bot-

128

tle of water, some cookies, a flashlight, a first aid kit, a blanket, a penknife, and other items I can't recall, as Grandfather only allows me to take out the contents once a year to replace those food items about to expire. In the middle of the night, when we least expect it, he blows a whistle and Grandmother and I must get out of bed, grab the backpacks, and run to the door, ready to evacuate. Each time he calls for this barbarous operation, the neighbors come out and band together to protest the ruckus instead of complaining. "Worthless cowards," he replies to them.

The emergencies could be anything, including earthquakes, landslides, fires, floods, bombings, gas leaks, or unknown dangers. The evacuation plan includes removing Great-grandmother, but we never rehearse that. Grandfather has everything planned. He shows us the diagram and then questions us. We respond rapidly and correctly, even though Grandmother insists that in spite of these absurd rehearsals, the day that it really happens she's not about to risk herself to save the old woman, who made her life miserable when she was still rational.

My grandmother's brother lives alone in the countryside. I've only seen him once. Grandmother tells me he was once the handsomest man in the region, that women pursued him. But he never married because the parents of the girl he loved rejected him. Not long ago their paths crossed and the two of them began to feel the love of so many years ago. But she was married, so they concocted a plan: She'd tell her husband she was going to the countryside to visit some friends, but they'd take the train together and get off at the station, where my uncle would take her to his home and finally they could love one another.

"*Love* one another," my grandmother says and savors the word while I continue to sew on buttons.

"Stop babbling, I can't hear the news," my grandfather shouts with the television blasting in the background.

"They got on the train pretending not to know one another, sat down next to each other, and finally could hold hands, gaze at each other, and think about the hours to come," my grandmother says sighing. "But halfway through the journey, she died. Without any warning, without pain, without any sound. She simply stopped breathing. Perhaps emotions overwhelmed her and caused a heart attack," Grandmother states sighing again. "He waited until they arrived at the train station and he got off the train before telling the attendant that the woman in the seat next to his seemed ill. And he left her there, dead, but with their honor intact. That's what you call a family secret," Grandmother concludes.

"So tell your alcoholic father and your other uncle about this liar, " Grandfather exclaims. "And your homosexual cousin."

One of the recipes that I read to Great-grandmother is called "Meringue Custard." It's the one I most love reading and imagining. Scoops of snowy white meringue on custard that's pallid and yellowish. I read the recipe to her over and over:

Ingredients:
One liter of milk
Eleven egg yolks
200 grams of sugar
vanilla
cinnamon
lemon zest

Preparation:
Heat the milk with the vanilla, cinnamon and lemon zest. Beat the yolks with the sugar. Allow the milk to cool and then add the beaten egg yolks, stirring continuously. Then place the mixture in a bain-marie, all the time whisking the ingredients. Once you're confident that it's set, remove it from the stove. Pour the mixture into parfait glasses or a deep ceramic dish. Top with syrup over scoops of meringue. Refrigerate and serve the same day.

In the kitchen, I begin to heat sweetened condensed milk and Grandmother takes over. We take a glass to Great-grandmother, who can barely swallow. The yellowish liquid trickles down around the wrinkles of her mouth, but she emits sounds as her tongue attempts to capture the cooled milk. She looks up and her eyes are watery, like those of Milu, her dog.

Two men approach me on the street, as I'm walking to school.
"Where's your mother?" they ask out of nowhere.
"At home," I respond.

"That's your grandmother," they reply.

"She's my mother, has always been my mother," I tell them emphatically.

"Have you not seen how old she is?" one of them mocks me as he grabs my arm.

"She's not an old woman! Your mother must be the old one!" I scream as I struggle to wrest myself from his firm grasp. Then I begin to run home. I couldn't attend classes that day, even though my grandfather was furious. Let him scream.

When the coup d'etat happened, my grandfather had already been retired for a couple of months. They requested that he retire before he turned fifty. According to my grandmother, it was a shame, even though she thinks more about the pension and not the career that he'd had in telecommunications. A few more years, and he would've been promoted to another level, a larger check at the end of the month.

"Stop complaining," he tells her. "And don't even think about bad-mouthing the glorious army of Chile. The only one to blame is your daughter. She blacklisted me. And never say *coup d'etat*," a rather military pronouncement.

My grandmother dreams of having a Japanese garden: "It's my most fervent desire." She well knows she'll never have one, but she longs to at least visit one and remain gazing at it until she's exhausted. According to her, a Japanese garden mirrors the universe: it's a vast sea filled with rocks that represent mountains and islands, and there's always a bridge that unites all the spaces and a teahouse where you can stretch out listening to the songs of birds and the sound of tree branches swaying in the breeze. She'd be content with a mirrored pool, with lotus flowers floating on top and several koi swimming just beneath the surface.

"That would be a crappy mess," Grandfather responds. "Plants rotting in the green water, dead fish, our property filled with undesirable critters, and you'd strut around naively, stupid woman."

"Without a kimono."

"And with your teacup covered by moss." He roars with laughter while imitating her delicate gesture with the raised pinky, drinking from an invisible porcelain teacup.

I tell my schoolmates about the accident that we almost had in Talc-ahuano. An enormous ship was swiftly coming directly at us and I was at the helm. My uncle shouted, "Turn starboard, turn starboard!"

I have no idea how I somehow knew he was shouting, vehemently and without a doubt, to turn toward the right. The yacht veered to the right and heeled over to the point of nearly capsizing, avoided the threatening keel of that enormous ship which, quite simply, hadn't seen us.

I speak in a serious, calm and convincing voice. They all believe me. Moreover, in their pupils I can see the dead whale beached on the shore that I described to them. They imagine and visualize the school of fish as a dark and dazzling speck in the sea, and the frenzied seagulls hovering above, block-ing out the still luminous afternoon. Two black blotches, one in the sea and the other in the sky. And from above, one dark shadow descends and devours the other. Both are now fused in a bloody state of confusion. So much noise made by all the shrieking, splashing, and flapping of wings.

One of the ladies, Ema, enters the house and declares, "Filthy pigs, all of them are filthy pigs. There were boys in the small plaza engaged in nasty behavior," she tells us, "in broad daylight, without any shame."

"Perhaps they were with the guy from the corner store," I say to her. "He's disgusting, always sniffling and wiping his nose with the sleeve of his shirt. "

They chase me out of the sewing room and tell me not to get in-volved in grown-ups' matters. "The adults' nasty acts are from the waist down," my grandfather laughs and slams the door so I'm forcefully shut away in my room.

Outages are not emergencies. They don't belong in the same category as those incidents that truly qualify as emergencies, when I have to grab my backpack. "Stay in bed and fall asleep as if nothing is happening," my grandfa-ther insists. However, if the outage begins when we're eating, he lights two can-dles: one on top of the amazingly silenced television and the other above the windowframe in the kitchen. Grandmother has to turn off the gas, and if she's cooking something, it's put away for the following day or later on, when the lights finally come back on. He takes his regulation flashlight and goes outside to confirm with the neighbors that, indeed, we are all without light.

"It was an assault on one of the high voltage towers," he pronounces with certainty.

There's always someone who has a battery-operated radio and they all gather around it, listening to the metallic voices of newscasters who are equally ignorant and know nothing yet never stop talking and end by blaming the recently created central system that coordinates the delivery of electricity throughout almost all of Chile.

We go shopping at the flea market. Clothing hangs overhead on high hooks and is heaped onto tables. Grandfather's fond of antiques. He always ends up buying a photograph in tones of sepia, with boats, bars, or very elegant women.

"I was there, I had to have been there," he claims. He also purchases bronze items, from the mines in the north or from the salt mines. When they were younger and my mother was a child, they transferred him to Arica, Iquique, Antofagasta.

"The north, always that gray, arid north, with the hills coming down upon us," Grandmother says.

"You never understand anything, you never understood anything," he proclaims with nostalgia for his military assignments in those zones.

"The women in the north have no morals. They couldn't care less if a man's married," Grandmother mumbles.

"The same with women in the center and the south," Grandfather responds. "There are bitches everywhere. It's not a matter of climate or landscape."

"Everyone says she's not your mother but your grandmother," Raquel tells me. She's actually the one that thinks that and pretends to be speaking on behalf of the others.

"Nor is he your father but your grandfather," she insists.

I reply to her calmly, softly, "Perhaps you are unfamiliar with the story of Elizabeth, the Virgin Mary's cousin? Those of us born to older parents are miracles, chosen ones. We're born blessed, without original sin. With a special mission like that of St. John the Baptist." She gives me a puzzled look, but finally believes me.

"John the Baptist was screwed for being horny," Grandfather insists. "He wound up decapitated for being a horny bastard. That's why I refuse to call him a saint."

133

Under my bed I keep the music box I took from Raquel's house. I play it when Grandmother's at the sewing machine and even though I find the silly plastic ballerina spinning on her metallic stick boring, I'm not about to return it.

The nuns' shoes are flat and unattractive with rubber soles. They wear long, heavy skirts, and straight blazers buttoned up to the neck. The female teachers wear a smock, elegant shoes and make-up. But they greet the nuns reverentially, as if they had some divine authority. I do the same because it's part of the education we receive.

Protest marches are beginning in our neighborhood. From every neighborhood emerges a band of individuals that converge in Plaza Italia and head down the tree-lined boulevard. Soon special forces are dispatched, unleashing tear gas and streams of water. I watch them on television and try to spot my mother. It's obvious that she won't be there, I'm aware of that, but I still search for her among those in the crowd, while my grandfather insists that everyone that opposes the mandates of Pinochet should be killed. "Spawn of the Indians," he proclaims.

At the clinic, they give me a vaccination due to an outbreak of flu. Grandmother's sufficiently elderly, so she's spared the needle's prick. In the waiting line, a woman loses consciousness and others catch her as she falls. They fan her with whatever they have in their hands. A nurse approaches and mumbles, "As if we didn't have anything to do these days, the hysterical one faints."

"Many people have become cranky in this country," my grandmother complains. "Every day there are more bitter, miserable individuals."

"They already killed your father. She's next," a guy whispers in my ear. He keeps walking and at the corner gets into an car with other men and a woman.

Sundays it would be impossible to miss going to church. Grandfather always wears a suit and tie. I put on a blue dress with a white collar that my grandmother sewed specifically for church and special occasions. We sit in the second row of pews, which is for those who arrive on time but are not considered important enough to occupy the first row, which is reserved for distinguished individuals. Never has anyone of importance arrived. When just anyone comes and sits in the front row, Grandfather states that even though they're shameless lowlifes, we're going to respect the rules of the House of God.

One day I find an abandoned missal and tuck it under my jacket. It has a pearl white hardcover with an embossed golden cross. A lady returns from communion, her head bent like a penitent's, and looks everywhere, but I have no way of knowing if she was seated next to me a while ago and carelessly lost her missal.

Pollution has increased dramatically in Santiago and they now prohibit driving cars with certain license plate numbers on alternating days of the week. Taxis and buses are also subject to the restriction. The drivers are immobilized and take advantage of those days to tune up and repair their vehicles. Auto body shops are filled with men that converse and check out motors.

Grandfather arrives late to lunch on those winter days when there's a lot of smog. "The fresh air is heavy and forces down the black cloud of pollutants," he explains to me. Grandmother coughs and her eyes water, but I believe that's because of the kerosene heater. It emits smoke but Grandfather refuses to buy a new one because he isn't a millionaire and isn't about to humor some disgruntled old women who complain about freezing to death because of a few clouds and are incapable of enduring a breeze.

There was an assault on a bank. They say it was the terrorists and not common delinquents. I'm fearful of seeing my mother on the news, but I don't say a word. It's my grandmother who murmurs that she hopes to never see her involved in any illegal or reckless activity. That's how she speaks, minimizing her fear by lightening the tone of her words. Grandfather insists that women don't take up arms. "The extremists keep them to cook and fetch water. How stupid are they?"

The teachers say that copying on quizzes is a sin, and even if they don't eventually catch us in the act, God sees everything and will cast down a divine punishment upon us. I don't copy, I simply look over their backs to see the answers of the others and compare them with mine. I place my forearm over the pages so no one can see my answers and be tempted to copy them and be banished to hell.

Divine punishment comes in all forms and some can be very cruel and even seem disproportionately unjust. But God doesn't tolerate deceit, lies, and many other things that infuriate him, and his wrath falls mercilessly upon humans that attempt to outwit Him.

Grandmother kneels on the floor and marks for basting with pins she holds between her lips. One by one, she inserts them in the fabric. At times I sit next to her and hold a pin cushion so she can remove them more easily. She tells me that women don't like children in the sewing room, but I behave properly and quietly so they're not perturbed, and they often smile at me.

The Virgin's saint day is in July. Even if it's raining or we're all sick with a cold, it's obligatory that we make the pilgrimage up the hill to the sanctuary. There stands the imposing white figure, stiff as a meringue torte.

Sometimes my mother sends me stickers of animals inside her letters and I place them around my nightstand. She could send me a bicycle or money to buy one.

What I most want in this world is to have a bicycle.

I'd even settle for skates.

Maybe not.

They always give me clothes for my birthday. Dresses and blouses that Grandmother has sewn, and sometimes a pair of shoes. Once my uncle sent me a huge book, hardcover, with the title *Short Stories of Yesteryear*. It's obviously been used as the pages are well-worn.

I like to look at myself in the mirror. I know I'm beautiful and that my hair is, indeed, something vey special, thick and long. Even though it's always forced into two tight braids by my grandmother, when night falls, I let it loose and examine how the light reflects in each strand. I brush it vigorously until it becomes electric. If it's cold, I dig my hands into the mane, wrap them around my neck, and everything becomes warm.

On the street, a woman approaches and tells me she has a package for my mother. She explains that they were schoolmates in high school and also in university. She has something in her bag that my mother asked her to keep as long as she could.

"I'm going to live outside Chile so I can't keep it any longer," she says in a singsong voice. Nearby there's a white car with men inside. I respond that my mother's at home and that she should come with me. I point to the silhouette of my grandmother in the window and she insists that's not my mother.

"Why don't you keep it and when you see her, or speak to her by telephone, tell her that you have this very important package."

Sincerely astonished, I tell her that she's confusing me. "That's my mother—the only mother I've ever known—so that package can't be ours," I tell her, shaking my head from one side to the other.

Every year before spring arrives, Grandfather insists that I need to learn to dance *cueca*, the national dance of Chile. "If you're Chilean, you have to dance *cueca*. If you don't dance *cueca*, you're not Chilean. It's as simple as that."

So Grandmother sews me a dress with a lace petticoat, an apron, and an embroidered handkerchief. Grandfather stands in front of me and challenges me with his white kerchief. "Resist me. Tell me no," he pants as he comes on to me.

Once the music behandergins, he circles around us in that imaginary square in which we meet, the timid, vulnerable young girl, and the harsh, stubborn man. "Come on! Continue. Smile, flirt, but tell me no? No. Don't be prudish like your mother. She always said no, not with you, not with just anyone."

I don't hear my grandfather as I dance: I concentrate on my feet as they quickly brush the floor in time with the music, in harmony with my bending waist, my kerchief waving in the air.

With makeup, I'm even more attractive. I rehearse the movements of my kerchief in front of the mirror. My twisting wrist makes it slither in front of my eyes and smile.

In a basket with scraps of fabric, Grandmother has hidden a framed photo in which my mother appears dressed in pink tights and a tutu, dancing on her toes.

Raquel's mother polishes her nails at the dining room table. The radio's blasting. You have to learn early how to be feminine so you know the tricks of conquest and beauty. She explains to us that a desirable woman is capable of frightening even the most enthusuastic men.

"What exactly is an enthusiastic man?" I ask her.

"Any man that finds you attractive. And should you no longer intrigue him, his enthusiasm dissipates, and he never returns." She laughs when she's finished talking. She then arranges our hair and allows us to paint our nails in the color we prefer. The music in the background continues, and feeling beautiful, we all dance.

Grandfather makes me scrub my nails with a stiff brush until they lose their precious pink color. My hands become reddened by the icy cold water, and with my skin so rough, I look like a washerwoman.

"So you don't learn to turn into a whore," he tells me.

On television they announce that another female terrorist has been apprehended. The killed her because she resisted arrest: She began to fire and the military, wanting merely to interrogate her, had no option but to gun her down. She and two others that accompanied her. They show a black and white photo of her face. Looking straight ahead, seemingly calm, quiet, she is young, much younger than my mother.

"Someone has to do the dirty work, get muddy and stained with blood," my grandfather insists. "That is what Pinochet does, a veritable soldier and man. A great man."

When I go to the dentist, they fill two cavities. Grandfather prohibits me from eating candy from now on, and I have to brush my teeth after every meal while he monitors the time. Five minutes, without a pause.

"I'm not a millionaire willing to pay the bills for a child too lazy to brush her teeth," he tells me.

From the dentist's office I bring home magazines: almost all of them are *Condorito* comic books. One afternoon I bring one home that is called *Burda*, and I leave it in grandmother's work space.

"Where did this come from? Surely a client left it here," she says, somewhat preoccupied, all the while checking out and copying the latest styles in clothing.

Just outside the high school, Mrs. Marta parks her cart with sweets.

They don't give me money to buy anything and I can only imagine that it's because they don't want me to eat sweets. But I converse with the woman and sometimes she gives me a caramel that sticks to my teeth and is sweet and juicy. One afternoon she doesn't arrive and her brother-in-law replaces her, an ill-tempered man. He doesn't respond when we ask him questions, but I hear him whisper to the nun in charge of gatekeeping.

"They detained and disappeared him. With your grace and understanding, Reverend Mother, I'm helping out so her business doesn't go under."

"There are no people disappeared," my grandfather insists. "We're still at war and there are casualties, which is totally distinct."

The nun called the cops and the cart with sweets and plastic dolls disappeared. "I don't want strange men at the door of my school," the nun explains to a teacher.

"One never knows," she responds. "To be distrustful is to prevent."

For the plebiscite, Grandfather and Grandmother vote *Yes*. Their friends and my uncles, and whoever else votes *No* is no longer their friend or relative. That's how things are: If you're not with my general, you're not with me. Of course he'll win, by a landslide, more than 70% of the vote easily won. The majority approves the new Constitution without any idea as to its content. But they're satisfied, relieved, and we continue to march forward to save our country from Communism, wars, chaos, and death.

I add stickers to my album and my grandfather goes out into the street to march triumphantly. Those that oppose are assaulted. Soldiers arrive and skirmishes ensue, but he returns content, with his eyes weepy from the tear gas and because he saw his president stand on the balcony and thank his loyal followers.

A nun sits me on her lap and asks me to explain why I have a black eye. I tell her that I ran into the open door of a cabinet, that it was an accident. That truly is how it happened. I wouldn't lie. That was the truth. I relish telling the truth with the voice of a liar, making them believe there's something horrendous behind it all, even though there really is nothing and I simply ran into something while scurrying around the kitchen.

I enjoy the fact that the nuns and teachers all look at me with compassion.

They have more sympathy for me because I'm attractive, studious and I never get dirty or scream. My nails are clean and transparent, my hair tied back, and my clothing impeccable. The beautiful girls evoke more compassion than the less attractive, disheveled ones. It matters less if something terrible were to happen to one of them, whereas there would be great concern if it involved one of the good girls.

"You're a very valiant young lady," they proclaim when they award me a prize. I know how to blush and smile demurely, as a well-mannered and humble girl is a blessing in these times.

They give silly prizes like animal-shaped erasers, cellophane-wrapped candy, or holy cards of the Virgin Mary and saints that gaze up to the heavens with devotion. They're dressed in weightless robes and their hands are grasped with fervor. Their eyes are bright and somewhat glazed, as if on the verge of tears.

"That's what's called ecstasy," my grandfather informs me. He relates the lives of some saints. I especially like the story of St. Ramon Nonato, whose mother died while she was pregnant with him and they removed him from the womb of the dead woman.

Many saints punish themselves, donning haircloth and flagellating their bodies as the only means of purifying the soul. Those who sacrifice themselves on earth will attain heaven, according to my grandfather. That's why, once a month, he fasts, not eating all day and then at 7 p.m., as the suns sets, celebrates his sacrifice with his nightly glass of wine.

In autumn, I walk upon the fallen leaves and they rustle with each step. When it rains, I put on my rubber boots and slosh through the puddles. My socks get wet as well, though I'm not sure if it's because of the rain or the dampness of the unlined boots.

"If you like, we could line them with mink," my grandfather grumbles when I take off my stylish socks and place them on top of the stove to dry. He puts newspaper inside the boots. My feet become stained with the ink to the point that I can distinguish the black letters.

My mother calls. It's very difficult to hear her because she's far away, in another country. She doubts that she'll return to Chile, as she won't be able.

"They had her corralled." Grandfather repeats, "*Corralled.* That word is perfect for her," and he likens her to a sow enclosed in a pigpen.

140

Underground is another beautiful word. I was born clandestinely when my parents were in hiding, posing as others and fighting the dictatorship. That's what my mother told me. "We sacrificed our identity for the cause, but we gave you another identity, a special one, valiant, predestined, the identity of one born in adversity and shadows."

"In the end, beautiful or unbecoming, words are merely words," my grandmother adds.

Some time ago they did the paperwork to make me the child of my grandparents. My mother is now complaining. Grandmother's response: "Over my dead body."

Grandfather screams in the background, "Let her come looking for her. Let her dare to come!" His voice is menacing. That's how he talks.

They detain the elderly woman who sells small packages accompanied by her grandson. She's crying as they escort her away. "What will become of my children? What will happen to my cats?"

The children go away. Her cats wander around the neighborhood and rummage through trash cans. One of them captures a mouse, kills and mangles it, and leaves it at our doorstep.

Next to the grocery store they install a Polla Gol kiosk. People line up to place bets. They also sell cigarettes and candy, which infuriates the owner of the grocery store because he doesn't want competition.

"This is my corner," he reiterates.

Grandfather says that people are stupid if they gamble. He only participates because he's a fan of soccer and wants to demonstrate all that he knows. But he never wins. At times he doesn't even come close to guessing half the results of the games.

"Now you can call me whenever you want," my mother assures me. She's in Sweden, very far away. Even though she doesn't understand a word of the language, she already has a job as a cleaning woman, she rides the bus and has met people. There are a number of Chileans there, but she prefers to interact with individuals from other places to clear her mind of some of the many reminders of her country. She's taking classes in Swedish where there are students from several countries, each chattering in their own language. Not only does it snow, but there's a freezing, gusty wind, yet the houses are still warm inside.

Grandfather refuses to talk with her. "I didn't raise you to clean toilets. Not just anyone can enroll in the Naval Academy. Let alone become an engineer. Not just anyone. Cleaning up the shit of others can be done by anybody."

I'm not sure if I like my mother's voice on the phone. It's rather hoarse and she doesn't roll the consonants like Raquel's mother does.

Madame Ema is losing her hair. Suddenly she becomes totally bald, loses weight, and becomes gaunt. She writhes with the pain in her stomach. "It's due to cancer," my grandmother explains.

The disease is devouring her. She relates that the worst pain is the humiliation in the hospital. The doctor makes her wait for hours and finally gives her pills to calm her and says, "The treatment didn't work. Go home and die peacefully."

Grandfather claims women get cancer because they're women. Too many hidden parts, decaying and contaminating vital organs.

The deliveryman from the grocery store leaves to work at the business next door. He went from his bicycle and deliveries to Polla Gol. With his elbows on the counter, he hands out flyers and forms and receives payment for bets and sales. When there are no customers, he converses with the neighbors and puts on the airs of a gentleman. He doesn't wear overalls now, but a blue jacket. The grocery store owner won't speak to him and if he's asked, he replies that the man is disgusting. Totally despicable. "And I won't say any more, as I'm a decent man and don't go around speaking vulgarities like that crude traitor."

The show called "Goals" is a wonderful soccer program. It highlights the best of all the games.

An envelope with photos arrives from my mother. In almost every one she's pictured with snow all around her. Too much snow. There's an immense river that runs through the city. On the banks of the river you can see the ancient city with colorful houses, one next to the other. And the snow covering everything. In spite of the cold, people are riding bicycles in the streets.

I'm still the only one without a bicycle.

"The Swedes descend from the Vikings, who were strong, brave men," Grandfather tells me. "I respect them for that. Even though they were looters and assassins."

At the end of every year we have an awards ceremony. I go up to the stage numerous times to receive the certificates that the nuns have tied with white or blue ribbons.

My grandfather exalts in the glorious barbeques found alongside the highway to the south. He finds a car and we go off to eat until we're full. I order French fries to offset all the grisly meat entangled in front of me among greasy sausages. Grandfather carves the pieces of meat and dark, curdled blood spurts everywhere. "Eat protein, you finicky kid," he says while forcing a fork filled with bloody entrails against my teeth.

They transferred my uncle from Talcuahano to Punta Arenas. No more sailboats for a quite some time. In Patagonia the wind is freezing and so strong that people have to hold on to a tree or a post to avoid being blown down. The trees that do grow in the barren land, when they haven't been pulled up by the root and have managed to resist, have twisted trunks and branches.

The ticket to Punta Arenas is too expensive, so just Grandfather travels and we women are left home in charge of the television. Two weeks without watching the news or listening to the radio blasting at full volume.

Grandmother is kneeling, marking a hemline. With pins held between her lips, she stretches the fabric with her two hands, folds it, and masters it. At some point, she falls backward. She stares into space, horrified, can barely get up, and just like that, with her gaze beyond us, tells us that she's swallowed a pin. The woman with the unsewn dress gives her water. "Drink plenty so the pin goes down," she says insistently.

I want to call the doctor but I don't know the phone number, nor that of the ambulance. Grandmother stands up and says, "It was nothing, my apologies, let's continue with what we are doing. It will take care of itself." She attempts to smile though she's still pallid, very pale. Even her wrinkles become transparent.

I run to the grocery store, but it's closed. In the adjacent store, Polla Gol, I ask them to call someone, to do something. The guy that was once the deliveryman laughs and tells me that whatever one eats, one shits. The others join in the laughter.

"I'm going to eat bread, lots of bread, so that it wraps around it and doesn't puncture my innards," Grandmother says. We bake her a cake, much softer and more delicious than bread.

She wheezes while she sleeps. The pin has nothing to do with that. It's because her lungs are weakened by having smoked while she was young and not so young. "Years with that disgusting vice," she remembers.

When Grandfather calls us from Punta Arena and I tell him about the pin, he begins to scream. "You're all worthless, you're not even capable of thinking this through if you can't imagine that a small, sharp piece of metal could go through vital organs. Do you know what an internal infection is? On what planet do you live? Haven't you learned anything in school? You're old enough to react, to think. Do you understand what it is to think?"

So we just leave him there, shouting on the phone, and we go to the hospital in a taxi.

We left Great-grandmother alone, since she never moves or complains.

Milu doesn't move or complain either. Nor does she relieve herself inside the house. "The day she begins to dirty the place, I'll shoot her," Grandfather has said.

The doctor says to Grandmother, "Are you out of your mind, Madame?" I clarify that she didn't do this willfully. Without responding, he glares at me and orders a nurse to take me out of there. They take my grandmother to get x-rays, bring her back, take her for x-rays again, and then leave her in an enormous room with nine other elderly women that groan in various ways. She's short of breath and looks at me terrified.

My mother isn't allowed to enter Chile. If Grandmother dies, she won't be able to come to the funeral. I'd have to live alone with my grandfather, cook the meals, clean the house, wash the clothing, clean Great-grandmother and go to school. It's too much work. Plus, if you're just the slightest bit neglectful, odors emerge from the filth: food that's spoiling, the garbage that accumulates. In the hospital they disinfect, but they're incapable of ridding the place of the smell of rotting flesh, the smell of the elderly.

"How old are you? Nine, ten? You don't need anyone to take care of you while your grandmother's in the hospital. I'll buy a return ticket. Close all the doors and don't cook anything on the stove. And take care of my mother. Check in on her three times a day. Your grandmother's in the Military Hospital. She's in good hands. The best, military hands."

The hose is the most useful item in the house. It's summer, so I

144

open the windows and from outside, I spray water. Once everything's soaked, I pass the mop over it. The house shines, although the rug makes a sound and emits a stream of dirty water when I step on it.

"What a tragedy, my dear," Madame Ema tells me. She can barely stand up, but she calls me to come by and pick up soup that she prepared for my great-grandmother. I eat almost all of it, as the elderly woman swallows very little and the soup's hot and delicious and I'm tired of eating bread and butter and salads of lettuce and tomatoes.

I open my grandmother's wardrobe and from within emanates a dusty and sweet smell. Dresses and more dresses. There's a box with two old hats, a black velvet one with a veil and another white one, made of felt. In another box, underneath the clothing, there are photographs of my mother. We look nothing alike. I'm more attractive. My hair is long and shiny, and I don't have her huge teeth or skinny legs.

In the upper part of my grandfather's wardrobe is his pistol and case with ammunition. Toward the rear, a shotgun. On top of the nightstand, a knife with a carved bone handle and a loaded revolver. "Well loaded," he claims.

Should my grandmother die from the swallowed pin and my grandfather perish in a plane crash returning home, what would they do with me? And with my great-grandmother? If I didn't let someone know she's there, she'd die of starvation and they'd find her decomposed body, withered like a dead tree limb.

I couldn't live alone with my grandfather. Nor with my uncle, which would be even worse. But I'm not about to travel to Sweden. So I kneel down in front of the Virgin Mary and pray the entire rosary. Essentially this entails an act of contrition, a reciting of the Creed, four Our Fathers, six ejaculatory prayers, six Glorias, fifty-three Hail Marys and a salutation to the Virgin Mary. I pray the entire rosary. They have to listen to me. The Virgin Mary or someone else.

The nuns say that if you pray the rosary daily, the Virgin Mary will fulfill the fifteen promises. I'd be content with the first promise: "Whoever serves me, praying the rosary daily, will receive whatever grace is asked." The others are for those are about to die, thinking about heavenly glory, hell, and the eternal soul. That's why so many elderly persons and so few youths recite the rosary. The Virgin Mary should make other promises, promises more grounded and practical.

The mailman brings me the bills and charges me the monthly fee. I have no money. I purchase everything on credit at the grocery store, and those few bills and coins that my grandmother kept in a jar are for emergencies. I'm accosted by the evangelists next door. They enter the house to see how I've been maintaining things, and without asking me about anything, they call the soldiers.

"An abandoned child," they denounce. "For days."

A female soldier takes careful note of all I say. I tell her my grandfather is flying back home, that I've been in the care of a neighbor, and there is no way of moving my great-grandmother. And that my aunt and uncle stop by daily to check in on us. Even though I describe them and give them a telephone number that I fabricated, they call the social worker. "It's protocol," they insist.

Regardless, I'm alone that night. Too bad the manual doesn't take into account bedridden elderly women. Only children. I give my great-grandmother scrambled eggs even though I was forbidden to turn on the stove. I devour eggs on top of a toasted bun with butter. It's so delicious that I fall asleep with the hunger that those very eggs awoke in me.

"Old bat." That's how my grandfather refers to the visitor after arriving home shortly after she was there. He's going to have to go before a judge because of me. But without an attorney, because he's not about to hire a charlatan when he can speak, loudly and clearly, for himself.

They discharged my grandmother, as the pin had passed without damage to her internal organs. The x-rays very clearly showed that the threatening pin had, indeed, passed. Grandfather admonishes her, "Don't tell me about it again."

"Nobody defrauds me," Grandfather screams at the taxi driver as he takes us home from the hospital. And he pays a different amount than that indicated by the taxi meter. Grandmother is healthy but jaundiced.

Grandfather stands behind me. Leaning on the door frame, he indicates what I should do. "Cut it and peel it just so. Clean your hands often with this rag. Use less detergent. Don't be wasteful."

He doesn't touch anything in the kitchen. "That's not the domain of men," he clarifies. He removes Great-grandmother's tray and I take a tray to my grandmother.

"I shouldn't be in bed if I'm healthy and sound of mind," she complains. I hug her and she smiles.

My mother sends photos from Sweden: Malmo, Gotland, Goteborg. And from cities in other countries: Helsinski, Oslo, Riga. She travels from one place to another wearing a heavy coat, hat, and gloves. She appears overweight under so many layers of clothing. Grandfather tells me that they eat chocolate and drink vodka because of the cold. She's no longer a cleaning lady, but a guide for tourists from Latin America visiting the city and its surroundings. Too often an enormous Swede with a moustache appears in the photos. "Your mother has always known how to adapt," my grandfather tells me.

When he thinks that we're not watching, he stares at the photos.

My cousins come to Santiago and stay with us. They've always gone to the home of their other grandparents, but that's no longer possible.

"My mother-in-law is depressed," Grandmother explains to the women that stop by the sewing room for alterations and new clothing. She tells them all the same thing. And that for two weeks she won't be able to assist them because the children have come for several medical and dental appointments, among other things.

That's another secret in my family. Aunt Margot's mother has attempted suicide several times. She swallows pills, turns up the gas, and cuts her wrists. Then she improves and begins cleaning energetically, goes out shopping and incurs major debt, invites friends and puts on a party. Then a couple of weeks later, she collapses on the bed crying, unable to get up. For days she doesn't bathe or talk to anyone. They give her pills, but they're not always effective. They subject her to electric shock therapy. It's a rare illness. Maybe that's why Martin was born with Down's Syndrome, having come from a family with so many defects.

But she doesn't throw herself from the twentieth floor or in front of the metro. Nor does she shoot herself in the mouth. "Theatrical, like all women," my grandfather claims. "When a man wants to kill himself, he goes and shoots himself without a word."

"I'm not fazed by any of it, not a bit. And they're not going to disrupt my schedule for even a minute," Grandfather grumbles.

If his son were to come, he'd let him sleep in his bed and he'd sleep on the sofa. But the children are a pain in the ass.

147

The eldest of my cousins doesn't use the bathroom. He relieves himself on the plants in the garden. He couldn't care less if people walking by see him. His younger brothers imitate him and the three of them gather beneath the Japanese maple, stand erect, tilt back a bit, and aim for the tree trunk, producing three curving, golden lines.

They also ask me to show them how I do it, crouched down over the ground. They tug at my skirt when I refuse, and I run to complain to Grandmother. My eyes become brilliant, teary, and they're punished, including Martin, the little one with Down's Syndrome. *Down* signifies below. A symptom of inferiority. I don't understand why that term is more respectful than Mongoloid, as that word comes from a distant, important country.

"Silly, *Down* is the last name of a doctor," my older cousin tells me.

Grandfather raps the children on the head. He runs his tongue over his knuckles and strikes them on the head. They run around, rap on the head. They yell during the newscast, rap on the head. They laugh at the dinner table, rap on the head. Predictable, no variation. They emit a brief, contained shriek and then move away to continue what they were doing. The boys don't learn a lesson and Grandfather can't understand why his knuckles don't stop anyone.

"I'm not interested in teaching them manners, I simply want them not to bother me," Grandfather alleges when Grandmother scolds him.

"What would our daughter-in-law say if she found out?" she sighs, short of breath. Ever since she swallowed the pin, she's begun breathing more deeply, painfully. "Women always talk. For no reason. Be grateful that you've been given more males."

The bomb explosion in the supermarket breaks the store's front window and people passing by begin to loot the merchandise. Soon others arrive to rob the store. The national police arrive to disperse the crowd, but they're not able to recover anything. The thieves took off running, their arms filled with merchandise, with no intention of paying a dime.

"Germs and bacteria are taking over these sneakers. They have a life of their own, multiplying exponentially." Grandfather submerges them in a bucket of water, detergent, and Clorox. He also immerses my sneakers, although they merely smell of rubber. The four of us kneel down in the patio to scrub and rinse the shoes. They come out clean and are placed to dry in the sun. Meanwhile we walk barefoot and jump around, feeling freed from restraints. The next day they're dry and stiff, the inserts scrape our soles and the new wrinkles hurt our feet. He states that if he hears even the slightest complaint, he'll make us wash them again.

Upon awakening, we find Great-grandmother dead. The last one to see her alive was Grandmother, when she fed her. Night fell and at some moment she stopped breathing. She doesn't have the sheets grasped among her fingers nor a look of fear. She was the same as always, her eyes wide open, though perhaps a bit smaller, more withered and jaundiced. Grandfather leaves to make the funeral arrangements. He walks toward the door with tearful eyes and the checkbook in his hand. "The best for my mother," he proclaims.

My cousin with Down's Syndrome stares at her body, surprised, unable to react. He walks away frightened. I start to laugh and he relaxes and laughs with me. The others also break out laughing, trying to hide their nervousness. We're roaring with laughter in that small, foul-smelling room when my grandmother enters with some neighbors and slaps all four of us. "Heretics," she proclaims, "the dead are sacred."

Flowers are sent by the evangelist neighbors, those at the grocery store and Polla Gol, my grandfather's army buddies, the friends from the sewing workshop. The neighbors that barbeque don't send anything. My uncle calls from Patagonia and explains to his sons that this is the law of life, that we're all destined to die. One of the sons asks him if he, too, will die, and he responds in the affirmative, "Yes, one day. "The youngest son whimpers, "My mother? No. Not my mother." Another one says, "I don't want to die." And the night ends with a sea of tears until my grandmother brings ice cream and my grandfather turns on cartoons on the television.

I always saw my great-grandmother in a night shirt. Celeste blue flannel with a white bed jacket with celeste blue garter belts. But her armoire is filled with clothing smelling of moth balls. Grandmother rummages through the clothes: this fabric is still good, I can use it, these buttons are of the best quality, these shoulder pads will be useful. She places all the remaining clothes in black garbage bags and she donates it to the parish church. She keeps a black coat with a brown leather collar, that almost looks like a dead squirrel wrapped around her neck.

A woman visits us. She is young and beautiful, perhaps not so young and beautiful. This paternal aunt sits down on the sofa and while the tea gets cold, she tells us that, after the military coup, she had to go into exile.

"The military pronouncement," my grandfather clarifies. She nods in agreement and continues telling us that she was in France and Cuba. Now she has returned from exile and wants to meet me and introduce me to her relatives.

"Who are they?" grandfather demands to know. She replies that her husband is French, as well as their son, that her sister has always lived here but never dared to leave.

" She also has children. You have a total of four cousins," she tells me smiling. I have no paternal grandparents. They died before I was born, before the coup d'etat, before all of this. They were traveling in a bus that went over a cliff and they found them in an embrace among the remnants of metal.

My aunt brings a photo album. My father when he was a child, in shorts and a striped shirt. It's obvious that the clothing is tight, that he's grown more quickly than anticipated. When he's older, he has dark, shiny hair, an enormous mustache and is lanky. He almost always appears with a furrowed brow, especially in the photos in which he's giving a speech with his hand held high.

"We were so close," she says. "I so admired him." He was her older brother, but now she is much older than the man in the photos.

"Those people are not trustworthy and, for the time being, you'll not be going anywhere without us. They want to brainwash you. They must think I'm an idiot," Grandfather says.

My mother continues to insist that I visit her. She promises that she's going let me return from Sweden, that she'll provide them with all the guarantees they need. She also tells them to take me to see this new aunt and her family.

"They're her blood relatives. He's her father," she says, weeping. Grandfather tells her that he won't put up with so much crassness.

"Let's kindly stop relating stupidities every time we speak on the phone with her."

They fix vegetables and salads at Raquel's house. Her mother's never going to gain weight because she counts calories. She insists that we don't just have bodies, but that we are our bodies and if we damage them with fat, we're changed into a greasy, amorphous mass that no man will desire.

"An overweight woman becomes invisible to men," she concludes.

My father is always going to be lanky and youthful. On the other hand, my mother keeps gaining weight and getting older.

They killed two policemen. One died in the assault and the other in the hospital. "They're martyrs of the institution," Grandfather insists. "Martyrs for the patriotic cause."

They conducted a raid and five extremists died. They began shooting and refused to be defeated; they knew they wouldn't be coming out alive. "They brought it on themselves," Grandfather alleges.

I still have not menstruated. One day they'll scratch me and scars will form, or they'll take me to a hospital and inject blood-filled syringes into me. Blood comes out blackish from veins, red from the skin. Raquel's mother says that we women must cure our wounds as scarred skin chases men away.

"They're repulsed," she explains, if they see scars when we gesture as we speak. Truthfully, it's pretentious, but we cover ourselves with cream to soften our elbows and knees. We paint our fingers and toenails and then finish it off with more cream. She proclaims that the summer sun is our enemy, fatal for our skin, so we don't dare go outside without our wide-brimmed hat.

The nuns insist that to blame is terrible and can even be a sin. When we go to confession we can tell the priest everything, absolutely everything, so I take advantage of that to relate everything bad about others.

Many men in Sweden are blond and named Lars. The one who married my mother is named Lars, and has hair like dry straw.

"A handlebar moustache," Grandfather grumbles.

Lars sends me a card in which he writes that he wants to meet me, that he loves my mother dearly, and that he will love and care for the son my mother is expecting. He confesses that he'll love me when he meets me. He writes in Swedish, and my mother annotates the translation.

"He speaks like a kindergartner," Grandfather says. "Just because he's tall, blond, and European doesn't save him from being a moron."

"Chileans are complicated," Grandfather tells me. "They admire foreigners as if they were a superior race. But there's no reason for us to feel inferior in their presence. We live in the most beautiful country, with a varied landscape, and a history filled with bravery and fearlessness. A nation of heroes, even though there are so many Indians still roaming in the south."

The first Saturday of the month, Grandfather spends the day instructing civilians, teaching them to be reservists should a war occur. "Another war," he adds, "because defeating communism has been a war."

Grandmother devotes her time to knitting cerulean blue sweaters and says that once the child is born, she'll have to travel to see him. She cannot have a grandson and never see him; it's impossible, she insists. Grandfather states that no one will take a damn dime from him to travel to an inhospitable, frigid country, with that shitty language.

I'd prefer a bicycle before an airplane flight.

Madame Ema is so thin that her nose appears enormous and eagle-like. Grandmother and I visit her, bringing her stews she can't eat. She barely takes two bites and begins to vomit into a plastic bowl.

"I want to receive the last rites so I can die in peace," she says.

"She wants to receive the last rites in order to die in peace," her sister repeats. She's an enormously overweight woman who stays with her to take care of her. The daughter of the plump women is also there, another overweight woman with greasy hair and a wide, wrinkled mouth.

Madame Ema looks at photos from her youth. "What did I do to stop being what I was? she asks. "At what point did everything change?"

"Time inevitably changes everyone," Grandmother comforts her, everyone.

"Evil of many, consolation of fools," my grandfather tells us.

The hefty women clean out Madame Ema's closet. There are no longer decorations and on the walls one sees the outlines of the paintings they've removed. Grandmother says that they're scavengers, that even vultures wait until their prey is dead before stealing from them.

Even though she says that, I still take some white linen handkerchiefs with green embroidery.

Grandfather insists that no one is going to demolish the room that he built for his beloved mother. "Go to the market to buy your damned herbs. The patio will remain exactly like it is."

He stores his tools and his shotgun there. He builds a carpenter's workbench and hangs some wooden planks for shelving. He leaves everything in order and organized, but he never returns.

Then the earthquake happens. It's Sunday, it's dusk on a warm evening when everything sways. Nothing happens to single-story houses. Not even the teacups in the cabinet with glass doors are tipped over. But in other cities the churches have been razed and many people have been crushed and killed. The cracks that appear in the bricks, in the thick walls seem like black serpents creeping along the borders, attempting to enter through the windows.

Grandfather goes away for a few days. "To help with the reconstruction," he says, "to rebuild the nation." He goes to the Santa Rosa church in Pelequen as part of a commando unit. I want to accompany him, but he tells me that classes are beginning and that men are not about to be taking care of bratty kids. They have to attend to their mission to lift the nation up once again.

The teachers and nuns become hysterical with each aftershock. Some of us dive under the desks and laugh. Others cry because they're stupid and don't understand that an aftershock isn't a real earthquake.

At school the girls park their bicycles on a small patio to the side of the entrance. Not all of them use locks. Not all of them take care of their bicycles. Some simply leave them tossed on the grass. I slip away during recess and ride one of them. I pedal down the narrow adjacent alley filled with garbage cans, discarded desks, and useless rubbish. I maintain my balance and ride in a straight line until I reach the end of that short and smelly alleyway. The wind caresses my legs and I manage to close my eyes for a second, and that brief moment makes up for the hours of waiting, the risk of being discovered, and having to confess to the nuns that I'm the only girl without a bicycle.

In the house in front of ours, where the grandmother that once sold drugs lived with her grandchildren, a couple with kids now live. She's young, but he's older, has bald spots with scars, and walks with a limp that he can't conceal. His left arm hugs his body because of a stroke.

"I should stop by to greet them. Who knows, it could be a new client," Grandmother says.

"I don't know how I'm going to get used to this neighborhood, if you'll pardon me, Madame. A block away I saw some youths beating each other, without provocation. It wasn't even night and there were the gangs. They've graffitied the walls, and the streets are blocked off. The jail attracts them like a magnet, as if they wanted to be inside. They're taking over the city, little by little, even from there. From the periphery, they continue to advance closer and one day they'll arrive at the center of Santiago."

"And, mind you, they are just beginning. May God rescue us."

One of her sons is my age. His mother calls him Tato. "Tatito, be careful. Tatito please bring the sugar bowl to this lady. Invite Manuelita to play with your toys." We go to his bedroom, where the walls are covered by bookcases. "I've read every one of them," he boasts. "They're almost all history books," he adds while stroking his firm thighs. "I am going to be wise historian, just like my father."

The neighbor tells grandmother that she'd been a student of her elderly husband. He was married at the time but left everything to be with her. It was an intense, passionate romance. She so admired him and would gaze at him in his classes and lectures. She listened to him strum songs of protest, his voice restrained and sensual. After they married, his wisdom wore off and she began to see all his defects, which sprouted like mushrooms. His lack of organization, his apathy, his stench, his reiterations, his withered body, his ineptitude. He never had an ounce of originality or creativity. He was entirely mediocre. By that time they already had two children. And then, with the coup, he went into hiding, even though no one was following him. He was able to remain employed by the university only by keeping a low profile and being obedient.

"It suits him to be squirming," his wife says. "And now that he's sick, what can we do? Put up with it, endure it."

Grandmother places her hand on the woman's shoulder and comforts her. "He 's lasted a long time, just like my mother-in-law. Eternal patients."

When we leave, Grandmother tells me that our neighbor lady is despicable as she reveals family secrets to the first person she meets. "She doesn't respect her husband," she explains to me. "There are certain things that are never said."

Raquel's mother has also instructed us that one should never use bad language because it shows a lack of respect for the individual listening and humiliates the one speaking crassly. "Self-abasement," she adds. For that very reason we never say bad words, insults, or anything aggressive. "That's what men do, especially rude, ill-mannered men."

"Speaking with a woman who swears is the same or worse than sitting at the table with a merchant marine," Grandfather asserts.

I tell my grandfather that the grocery store delivery guy that went to work for the store Polla Gol wants to become a merchant marine.

"Let that jerk desire whatever he wants," Grandfather responds, "but he's not the kind of person you'd invite to your home. Stupidity knows no limits," he adds.

I wash and iron the doilies that belonged to Madame Ema. I wrap one in silk paper, as grandmother refers to tissue paper. I take it to Raquel's mother as a gift. She lingers looking at it and and then asks if my grandmother gave me permission to give it to her. I bought it, I reply, and while I speak I notice a greasy stain that I hadn't seen and the doily appears old and worn, the thread faded around the edges. "I bought in a store that sells used items," I add. She forces a faint smile.

Raquel's younger brother looks at us and laughs. He thinks we don't see him hiding things. We pretend to search for them with desperation and he laughs and laughs. He's three years old, also red-headed, with dark skin and freckles. The dimples in his cheeks and chin make his face resemble the cracked top of a *Pan de Pascua*.

His mother gazes at herself in the mirror, undoes her blouse, and declares, "It's that child's fault that I lost the voluptuous cleavage I once had."

Raquel has a pink bicycle with a white basket in front decorated with plastic flowers. "A Barbie-style bike," her mother tells us. She pedals down the sidewalk and rings the bell when she approaches me. Standing against the fence, I watch her come and go. She's assaulted by gusty wind and yet she doesn't teeter. Nothing stops her.

She can ride as far as she wants, pedaling until nightfall. But she only goes around the block repeatedly.

My mother's baby is born. It's a boy and they name him Johannes, which is equivalent to Juan. Grandfather's name is Juan, so this was done in his honor. That means he can now forgive her. Not entirely, but at least somewhat. In the photos it's clear that my brother is going to be strong: his hands held tightly in energetic fists, he's chubby, with a ruddy complexion.

"As long as he's not baptized and continues to be a Moor, he's not my grandson," Grandfather insists.

I don't recognize my mother, who's gained weight and developed wrinkles in her neck from having bent over her baby boy so often. She also appears older with her hair cut short.

Grandfather no longer goes to the workshop. They're laying off people due to the recession and they can't pay him.

Raquel's mother says that an unemployed man's a disgrace because they don't know what to do around the house. Therefore, a woman should search for a husband who's hard-working, one who leaves early and arrives home late, exhausted. "That way, a woman is master of time," she concludes. "And for a woman, there's nothing more valuable than time."

Wasting time in concealing the passage of time.

Some young people were climbing over the barricades and burning tires when the National Police arrived. They caught two of them, wrapped them in blankets, doused them with gasoline, set them ablaze, and threw them in a ditch. Some peasants discovered them and took them to the hospital. The man died, but the woman survived— completely burned, but alive.

"They went too far," Grandmother declares.

"And just what were they doing with those firebombs? Playing marbles?" Grandfather shouts.

The hot water in the bathtub is hard to endure. I get in a little at a time. My feet can tolerate it, then my thighs, but I don't manage to sit down in the tub until later, when my legs are red and the steamy heat rises and mists the white tiles. Skin that has been literally burned, the pain of skin with open wounds, burned all over, must be impossible to tolerate.

I remember the time I wanted to remove the toast from the toaster in the kitchen. I barely touched it, but my finger became swollen. I held it under cold running water and the skin turned red and began to throb.

Skin that's been burned has a distinct smell. What must burning skin smell like? How could you tolerate that carbonized odor knowing that it emanates from your own body?

I speak with my mother by phone and she tells me that electricity hurts as badly but doesn't leave traces. "When you come we're going to be able to talk about so many things. Do you remember what I've told you in my letters? Do you read them from time to time?" She speaks anxiously. She wants to hear herself, she wants me to hear her, and she wants me to answer in the affirmative to everything, but I prefer to remain silent and leave her waiting for a satisfying response.

"She must be tired of hearing those Vikings talk. She wants to recapture her language," my grandfather says. "When one loses one's language, the nation is also lost, and without a nation, we are nothing, simply orphans wandering the land," Grandfather states.

There are more and more people loitering. Everyone talks about it. The nuns totally agree.

The prisoners' relatives wander around the neighborhood. They look at the houses and then tell the prisoners what they've seen. Once they're released from jail, they know which houses to rob. That's why Grandfather likes to keep the shutters closed and the curtains drawn. That's why our house is always in semi-darkness, even though it's sunny outside. The Japanese maple is green and surrounded by the stately, colorful flowers planted by my grandmother.

Grandmother and I go to the city's center to buy fabric. We arrive at the Plaza de Armas and walk toward the street called Rosas. That's where the shops are that sell the lace, buttons and adornments that my grandmother adds to the clothing she sews.

I wait in the doorwway while she looks through the books with samples. Outside two men that appear to be plainclothes policemen are escorting a man by the arm. They pass in front of me and I hear him beg, "Please, please, no." He speaks in a lowered, hoarse voice, like a stifled expression of anguish from his very core.

Grandmother pulls me inside. "Don't peer outside. It's dangerous out there."

Our new neighbor tells her son to invite me to their home to play Trivia. We sit at the dining room table while his father, with a swollen face, watches us from the sofa. Tato knows all the answers because he has the cards to read and memorize when he's alone. His father looks at him with devotion and emits some guttural sounds to celebrate all of Tato's correct answers.

157

Tato cheats and his father has no manners, so I hide a few cards under the rug or between the cushions or among the books every time I go there. His father sees me doing it, but he's incapable of speaking. Tatito will have to search for them.

Having Grandfather home every day is difficult, as he awakens early in the morning and then obliges us to get out of bed even though it's still dark outside. Before leaving for school we've swept the sidewalk, washed the dishes, made the beds, and taken down the dry laundry ready to be ironed. "Idleness is the devil's workshop," Grandfather tells us. He now has assigned me tasks for the weekend that I should do methodically, according to a strict time schedule. "Afterward, everything will be subjected to an evaluation." He adds, "With military rigor."

He doesn't have any tasks.

From snow-covered Sweden, my mother tells me to be patient with my grandfather. "He is what he is. One has to learn to accept him."

She refused to accept anything. She ran off whenever or wherever she wanted.

Perhaps one day Grandmother will grow tired of all of this and go away. Even she may leave. "Perhaps I'll be going away, leaving behind merely dust," is what she says.

We can no longer understand anything Madame Ema says because she's been given a lot of morphine. She speaks incoherently and whines like a cat. They call a priest and ask us to join them for the last rites. She's spread on the bed in anguish, and we stand around her looking at the priest, who rubs the palms of our hands with oil and invites us all to pray for her. "Hear us, Lord, we implore you," we reiterate time and again. No one wishes for her to continue to live, but the chubby women find solace in her death and believe that her soul, once released, will be carried to heaven. Since nothing is guaranteed, we should pray more fervently. I have no idea where so many people come from when someone's about to die.

There've been two explosions but in two different areas of the city. One occurs at 11:30 and the other at 11:38. One man has been injured, a grocery store was looted, and millions of pesos were lost because of the damage. "Vandals," my grandfather says. "Animals, Indians."

We all have Mapuche blood. That's what the books state and it's well-known. Grandfather insist that this doesn't apply to him because among his ancestors, there was never a whore who got involved with the Indians.

Madame Ema dies at night. In the early hours of the morning the chubby ladies begin knocking on doors to announce the news to neighbors, all of whom sigh deeply, but close their doors, go back inside and continue with their daily routines. Grandmother and I stop by to pay our respects. It's an open coffin, and I lean over it to see her. Her skin is taut around her face and her mouth wide open, with sharply defined and jaundiced features. It's the second time I've seen someone dead.

Grandfather makes arrangements with the Church and the priest. "Respect," he says. "It's not enough to show respect. You have to demonstrate it." He even hires a violinist, whom he pays with his own money. The mass is a somber, private affair. There's a white ribbon along the aisle from the first pew to the last. And flowers. "Fitting," he says. "She deserves it. Respect for the deceased, a final tribute."

The new neighbor attends the funeral. She arrives without her husband, as it's difficult for him to move about, or her children, because they don't like the neighborhood and have no interest in adapting to their new environment. They're hoping something happens and they'll be able to return to their former home.

Johannes is becoming more chubby and blonde. From one letter to the next, he's transformed, becoming more monstrous without anyone seeming to notice. Those around him smile and he responds with an enormous grin that's cut off by his chubby cheeks. "A solid chest," Grandmother insists.

I imagine that enormous child balancing on top of my mother's full breasts, that plump woman who reaches out and holds that chubby child and gazes at him with puffy eyelids, heavy with excess weight, a total mass of enveloping fat.

They try to kill Pinochet, but aren't successful, though several individuals accompanying him died.

"And now, indeed, the authorities are going to clamp down harshly," Grandfather says with satisfaction. "They're going to search for and find those in hiding. They're going to come down fiercely upon them, they'll see."

159

"I can no longer resist," Grandmother replies. "I have to go, I have to go. Any day now I'll die, without being able to embrace my daughter or know my grandson."

"Stop swallowing pins and you'll live for many years," Grandfather responds. "Far more than I'll be able to put up with."

Once again we go to the town center. We don't walk toward Rosas Street but toward Huerfanos, where there's a travel agency that sell passages to Sweden.

Grandmother warns me that we can't talk about these inquiries, that we have to hide the brochure they gave us with images of the old city, the museums, the snow, and the immense sea.

"I have some money saved," she explains to me. We stop by the bank and she reviews her current savings account balance. She still doesn't have sufficient money to purchase tickets, but she could buy me a bicycle with that money. And still have money left.

There's no way they can take me to Sweden. I don't want to go outside in all that snow to push that monstrous child's stroller and everyone standing there watching me. Not by bicycle nor by airplane. There's nothing to convince me to travel to that horrible country with its impossible language and enormous people that walk against the harsh north wind.

It's impossible for me to go there, so I leave the brochures peeking out from their hiding place, staring fixedly at the brochures until Grandfather gets curious. I find the courage to tell him that those things belong to Grandmother, and are not to be touched. It was inevitable that he'd give me a push and pick up those brochures. They don't even interest him, but he's not about to allow a foolish child give him orders.

He doesn't know I'm a brat who secretly tells her grandmother everything, a brat who pretends to be surprised when she sees the photos of the airplane and the old city of Stockholm. A snotty young girl who's never even had snot.

Exit the airplane, hug one another in the snow, get into the car, read the signs in an impossible language, arrive at her hitherto unknown home, hear the crying of her horrible child. Eat raw fish, sauerkraut, and dill pickles, staring at one another with no recognition. And that would just be first day. Those that followed would be the same or worse. Who knows how many days. And nobody mentions anything about the return flight home. Grandmother might lose herself among the unknown streets and freeze to death beneath the snow, slip on the precarious ice, or swallow something sharper this time. And my mother would never allow me to return, that's evident. Perhaps they've already spoken and it's all planned to leave me there, a conspiracy. Or Grandmother's tired of her situation at home and prefers to stay there forever. Or she's going to go crazy and want to stay there and enjoy the antics of her chubby-cheeked, *mestizo* grandson, and quite simply she's not going to return home. Nor will she allow me to return.

"I'm not going to that country. The decision is made."

Grandfather tells me that I'm not going to Sweden. "That refuge of communists. That's where all the communists in the world go into hiding." Also, those countries are dealing with an influx of blacks.

"Why don't they lift the barriers at their borders once and for all? Soon the Asians will arrive. I want to see their faces when their blonde daughters cross paths with an African or Asian."

Grandfather allows me to hug him, but he continues to rant.

"They think that accepting anything is democracy," he says. "It's merely the beginning of the age of decadence, of the end of Europe—like the fall of the Roman Empire—invaded by barbarians, by uncivilized people and inferior races."

And I hug him even more tightly.

I'd love to put a knife to my skin and make a cut, ever so slight, so I could see my blood for the first time. The blade's cold and hard, the point very sharp. I'd feel the metallic taste of the knife. Just slight pressure and a red line would split me in two: the me before and the me after air entered my skin.

We go to the movies. It's the first time that he's taken me anywhere in the town center. The illuminated marquee announces the title: *The Last Cabin Boy of the Baquedano*. It's a film made several years ago, based on a book by Francisco Coloane. When it debuted, I wasn't old enough to understand it, Grandfather said, but now I'm at an age to understand the story of a young man who abandons his school in Talcuahano, the port city where my uncle Jorge lived, to travel as a stowaway on a ship with the objective of finding his brother in Punta Arenas, the city where my other uncle lives.

"Coloane was one of the great writers of our nation," insists Grandfather, "because he rescued the identity of the far south.

"Don't be confused," he states with a firm voice. "Even though most of the writers are considered Communists, and at times their literary value exceeds their reputation."

"Don't judge without knowing all the details, don't be ignorant," he adds. "There are too many stupid people. I won't let my granddaughter become one of them, one among thousands."

On MacIver Street, close to the cinema, there's a tea shop. My grandfather orders a large dish of eggs with bread and I order a grilled ham and cheese. They bring me chocolate ice cream with shortbread.

"Eat, little girl," eat my grandfather insists.

The waitresses, dressed in typical German outfits, smile at him and he returns their smiles.

"This is my granddaughter," he states, with a gesture that only I'm able to interpret: pride in my fine manners, my reserved smile, and my hair, as we well know, shines more brilliantly than a gem.

They wrap up some pastries and marzipan dogs and cats. "They are for you, only you."

Even so, I give the head of a marzipan cat to my grandmother. A head with a reddish tongue and crimson wool around its neck. That stupid cat keeps smiling even though it's been decapitated.

I recite the names of cities from north to south and from south to north. I sit down with my grandfather to read about the great battles, and his booming voice vibrates with the battle hymns we sing because one should never lose respect for hymns, especially those that honor the nation.

I get up early. I'm familiar with the way the dawn breaks, bursting from behind the mountains and the harsh, dry geography of the east. Grandfather's pleased to see my silhouette against the morning light while I perform the first duties of the day. I do whatever he orders me to do and more. I take his shoes to the patio and shine them until they're lustrous. I sweep away the leaves in front of the house and run to the kiosk for the newspaper, which I leave next to his chair at the dining room table that my grandmother prepared the previous night. I turn on the television to watch the morning news. I serve him a cup of hot tea and he taps my head. It's a lot for him to show any semblance of affection.

While I'm seated on the floor shining his shoes, Milu installs herself next to me and stares at me with eyes similar to mine, wide and brilliant. I offer her no caress because she's a female dog that licks her owners, spreading infections. Her coat is progressively more sparse and stinky.

The two of us are going to be just fine, without Grandmother. That's what I need to say. I finally tell him that I'm not about to travel , that I'll stay there with him, remaining in my homeland like a true Chilean.

"Stop saying the same thing over and over. Shut up, and let me listen to the news," he says. But he doesn't scream at me. He no longer raises his voice.

I still have some of the marzipan cookies, and I give him the hind legs of a dog. He laughs and scarfs them down in one bite.

My cousins and some of my grandmother's friends stop by. They bring a torte to celebrate her birthday and to give her a fond farewell, as we are about to travel. I tell them they're mistaken: my grandmother's traveling alone. I'll be staying home to take care of my grandfather,

To get to the zoo one has to travel to Baquedano Plaza, walk toward the north until reaching the side of the hill, and then climb the slope. Little by little you begin to hear the shrieking of the monkeys and smell the foul odor of food fermenting in the cages. Grandfather's hand grips mine so tightly, firmly that it's impossible for me to get lost among the crowd. I cling to him.

My cousins run up the hill ahead of us. The one in the middle, with Down's Syndrome, carries a bag of popcorn that he throws into the cages while emitting shouts. He shrieks, gathers a fistful of kernels, and tosses them through the bars. He then runs to the next cage and repeats the routine, but only after having devoured some of the treat. His brothers follow him and imitate his actions. I, on the other hand, nibble some of the sweets and then offer them gently to the animals. My stride is elegant compared with that of my cousins, and I know Grandfather is watching us, understanding the difference between those unruly children and his discreet, refined grand-daughter.

Grandmother's suitcases are packed and closed, filled with winter clothing: woolen clothes, boots, scarves, and all the items she knit for this grandson that has made her as crazed as if a hunting horn had been thrust

163

into her. I unpack my luggage over and over again, and Grandmother continues to repack all my belongings until the day she tires of this and takes my suitcase and locks it in the bedroom where my great-grandmother once slept.

She's obsessed with my traveling with her. "You can go without me. I wish you all the luck in the world," I tell her with a smile.

And my smile is genuine, sincere. A captivating smile.

Rachel's mother tells us decent people never do anything grotesque; they behave in a smooth, subtle way. "A woman of distinction may act provocatively, but that's all," she says as she unbuttons her collar, fluffs up her hair, and flashes a sparkling smile between her thick, sensuous lips.

When Grandmother goes to the market, she takes the small cart that sounds like a rattle as she drags it along the winding sidewalk. Grandfather's at the home of neighbors helping them install an antenna on the roof that captures satellite signals and routes them to the television via a converter. They'll be able to watch several channels without paying a cent. Grandfather wants to see if it works before he orders a similar one from the free trade zone in the north. I have the house to myself. I open the glass doors of the cabinet and take out teacups, small plates, teapots and figurines. All of a sudden, I break one. I manage to get it back together, but it comes apart again, so I put some glue on the pieces to hold them and return the piece to its place. In a matter of minutes, there's not a single porcelain object undamaged, crudely repaired, and standing unstably inside the glass-doored cabinet. Since the light bounces off the doors' glass, the collection looks the same as before, without any defects. One day when Grandmother goes to serve tea, all of the handles on the teacups will fall off in their hands. It will be impossible for them to see my traces because many days, perhaps months, will have passed. There might even be an earthquake before then: this country's a seismic epicenter where quakes can happen at any moment.

I could do worse things, like take the kerosene from the heater and spread it around the roots of the Japanese maple. Within a few days the tree would turn dry and black, a shadow of its former self, with no way of recovering.

If so many people didn't walk down the street and peer through the fence at the beautiful flowers planted by my grandmother, I could get away with it. I'd have time to wash my hands and get rid of the odor. But such a frenzy of people walk down the sidewalk and turn their heads to peer at our house, without humbly lowering their gaze, as the nuns say they should.

I could also take Grandfather's pistol.

I have many more ideas. All of them subtle, as recommended by Raquel's mother.

She should be grateful that it's only a few teacups. They're rather tacky anyway.

I don't bleed nor do I have nightmares. At times I dream, but I soon forget them, because it would be inappropriate to walk around talking about them. Especially if they're dreams in which the wind intensifies the cold, and obese people with huge mouths gorge on raw fish and shout in an infernal language, their shacks surrounded by threatening forests where gray wolves await with open jaws, crouched among trees covered in filthy snow.

I hear screams. I leave the house so I don't hear them. It's a bright sunny day, flowers everywhere, and I walk to the corner to look at the food on the shelves in the store. I don't buy anything because I left without money, but I distract myself by ambling along the street, giving them time to stop screaming. When I return, they're still screaming at the top of their lungs. He shouts but she doesn't back down. Where did she get that harsh, raspy voice?

"We're leaving, no matter what you say. I'm not about to die like that."

Her voice was no longer wavering nor whiny, as she began to dominate his hoarse shouts, which finally yield to hers. He says nothing to lead me to believe he's defeated, but I know he lost this time. I'm surprised to learn what it was all about. She'd managed to put together the money or perhaps she asked my mother for it. But above all, he suspects that she no longer has a fear of flying alone nor is she intimidated by his objections. Whatever, she's not taking me with her. I'm staying behind with my grandfather. I don't want to see my mother or her enormous son, and especially not her mentally weak husband.

It's impossible that Grandmother's had enough and wants to get rid of me as if I were a bother, leaving me with a woman who's been tremendously deceptive. Maybe she doesn't like my mother. But the nuns have made it clear that I'm a notable girl, almost sublime, celestial, almost divine. Besides many who know me—Raquel's mother, Tatito's mother and the neighbors—congratulate her at having such a treasure. And they're not mistaken. It's merely a matter of seeing me to realize it's true.

Grandfather says that my grandmother's word rules, and if she wants to take me with her, I have no choice but to go. Neither Grandmother nor anyone else can oblige him to do anything, but in my case, it will be a different story.

"She's never been in charge," I reply. And then I add, "And you've never lied," although I whisper this so softly no one can hear me.

I am feverish, bedridden and vomit every time they speak to me. My bedroom reeks and I'm becoming ever more gaunt and pallid.

No one who's sick is allowed to travel, everyone knows that. The pilots aren't permitted to allow drunks or pregnant woman to board the plane. Nor individuals with infectious diseases, for fear they might infect the other passengers. The cabin might become a coffin if it's full of people with virulent infections. I remember perfectly well those words spoken by my grandfather. They've even made movies about it. If the pilot says you can't board, no one can oblige him to change his mind. Not even Grandfather with his old uniform and demanding voice would be able to convince him.

I still have some marzipan left, but I don't eat it. It becomes hard and brittle. I no longer take a bite of anything. Not even a sip of soup.

Grandfather says that I'm hysterical and that if I don't get over it, he's going to beat me.

"I'm not going anywhere. I'm staying here," I insist again. Grandfather shakes me, the first time he's ever touched me like that, and I begin shouting that I'm never going to forgive him, that one day I'll seek vengeance against him and he'll regret having sent me to that horrible country, so far away, populated by Communists and strangers.

He laughs. In the beginning he laughs, but that only lasts so long, just like my bicycle rides behind the school. He immediately regains his surly demeanor and grabs my face with one hand, his disfigured and rough fingers clutching my jaw, raises my head without realizing that he's choking me and snarls, "Shut up, bastard brat. Get out of here once and for all and take your pathetic abandonment with you. I can no longer stand to see you."

I don't play with the mercury from the broken thermometer like the younger ones would. I take the shards of glass and with no hesitancy cut myself, my pale and thin skin. How easily it opens, tinged a bright, limpid red. There's no way to stop the torrential flow of blood, warm and wet. The sun streams through the window and shines upon it, and burning sparkles emerge and silently spill out among the folds of the white sheets. How lovely is my blood, my patriotic blood, my virgin, untouched blood. It is, unquestionably, the most beautiful blood I've ever seen.

The Author

Beatriz García Huidobro Moroder studied pedagogy at the University of Chile and was a professor for thirteen years. She then earned a post-graduate degree in psychopedagogy. She served as Director of the Cultural Heritage Corporation of Chile for many years, overseeing projects such as congresses and conferences and the production of books on the investigation and dissemination of culture.

She is Executive Editor of Ediciones Universidad Alberto Hurtado. For years, Beatriz has been a literary critic, recommending a book each week on the radio program "Vuelan las plumas" ("Pens Fly") at the University of Chile. She is also a literary critic for the periodical *Mensaje*.

She has had novels for children and adolescents published with SM – Barco de Vapor, including *Misterio en La Tirana* and *Septiembre*. She won the contest "Santiago en 100 palabras" ("Santiago in 100 words"), which consisted of writing a short story with no more than 100 words. She has published novels with the publishing company Lom, including *Hasta ya no ir*, which was a finalist in the Sor Juana Inés de la Cruz literary competition (Mexico), which is open to women novelists throughout Latin America, *Nadar a oscuras*, and *El espejo roto*, among others.

The Translator

"I believe that translation is a veritable art form, wordsmithing that enhances greater understanding among cultures in this global society. Through my translations, I believe that I am establishing a threshold or a gateway to another culture, eliminating linguistic obstacles in order to provide access to culture-specific material. As a translator of Latin American literary works in prose, fiction and non-fiction, and poetry (Spanish to English), I consider myself a messenger of cultural and linguistic diversity. I str
ive to communicate through my translations a missive or message of tolerance and respect for diversity, a message of acceptance and celebration of the 'other,'"by shedding light on that which makes each language and culture so very unique."

Jacqueline Nanfito is Associate Professor of Spanish (Latin American Literature and Culture) at Case Western University in Cleveland, Ohio. She is also on the faculty of the interdisciplinary programs of Women's and Gender Studies and Ethnic Studies.

She is the author of several articles in Latin American literary journals, and has published several books on Latin American women writers: *Sor Juana Inés de la Cruz, El sueño: Cartographies of Knowledge and the Self* and *Gabriela Mistral: On Women*, a compilation and translation of selected prose writings about women by the Chilean Nobel Prize-winning poet, Gabriela Mistral. Other publications include a translation of micro-fiction by award winning Chilean female author Pía Barros, *Marks Beneath the Skin/Signos bajo la piel*; the translation of an anthology of micro-fiction by Chilean female authors denouncing violence toward women, edited by Pía Barros, *¡BASTA! + de 100 mujeres contra la violencia de genero/ENOUGH! 100+ Women Against Gender Violence*; the translation of seventy poems by the Chilean Jewish author and human rights activist, Marjorie Agosín, *The White Islands / Las Islas Blancas*; the translation of Agosin's prose poems about Anne Frank, *Anne: An Imagining ofo the Life of Anne Frank* and the novel *Fish Hair Woman* from English into Spanish, by the award winning Filipina author, Merlinda Bobis.